DEREK JOHNS

WINTERING

Complete and Unabridged

ULVERSCROFT
Leicester

First published in Great Britain in 2007 by
Portobello Books Limited
London

First Large Print Edition
published 2007
by arrangement with
Grove Atlantic Limited
London

The author wishes to thank
Methuen Publishing Limited for permission
to quote from Noël Coward's *Private Lives*
(Copyright © The Estate of Noël Coward)

The moral right of the author has been asserted

British Library CIP Data

Johns, Derek, *1948 –*
   Wintering.—Large print ed.—
   Ulverscroft large print series: general fiction
   1. Fathers and sons—Fiction
   2. Large type books
   I. Title
   823.9'14 [F]

   ISBN 978–1–84617–900–6

Published by
F. A. Thorpe (Publishing)
Anstey, Leicestershire

Set by Words & Graphics Ltd.
Anstey, Leicestershire
Printed and bound in Great Britain by
T. J. International Ltd., Padstow, Cornwall

This book is printed on acid-free paper

'If Winter comes,
can Spring be far behind?'

Shelley, 'Ode to the West Wind'

1

Billy raised his face to the sun, seeking its warmth. He passed under a canopy of trees which for a few moments turned morning into evening.

'We're having an Indian summer,' said Jim.

'What's an Indian summer, Daddy?' said Sarah.

'It's a summer that comes just when you think summer is over.'

'Is there a Cowboy summer too?' said Billy.

His father didn't reply, and Billy turned to look at him. He was wheeling his bicycle, and this seemed to absorb all his attention.

The road was lined with stinging nettles, dock leaves and Queen Anne's lace. When it dipped steeply towards the village, Sarah asked to hold Jim's hand.

'Take your brother's,' he said.

'I don't want to.' She tossed her hair, and Billy took this as a signal to run ahead.

'You're old enough now not to hold hands,' said Jim. 'And don't dawdle.'

'I'm not dawdling, I'm walking.'

'Yes, and slowly. Do you want to be late on the first day at your new school?'

'I don't want to go to a new school,' she said. 'I liked the old one.'

'We've been through all that. You have to go to a new school, just as I have to go to a new job.'

Billy climbed a gate that opened onto an empty field. In the hazy distance he could see a hill that rose sheer out of the countryside, with a tower at the top.

'Dad!' he shouted. 'Look at this. Is it a castle?'

'That's Glastonbury Tor,' said Jim when he caught up.

'What is it?'

'What is it? It's a hill.'

'But it must *be* something.'

'Well, there are stories. I don't really know them. You'll have to ask your new teacher.'

Billy was transfixed. This was the strangest hill he had ever seen, an impossible hill.

'Can we go there?'

'How?' said Jim, pushing off again. 'There are no buses for miles around.'

Billy was the laggard now, stopping at every gate to catch sight of the tor. How many fields would he have to cross to get there — ten, twenty? But then there were the cows. Billy wasn't sure about cows.

The school was a grey limestone building no bigger than a house, its walls covered in scarlet Virginia creeper, its only decoration a wrought-iron porch. To reach it they had to cross a stone footbridge over a stream. Alongside the bridge was a ford, the water a foot or so deep.

'Sit on the steps and wait for Miss Shute,' said Jim. 'I must get on.' He wheeled his bicycle up the slope past the church and swung onto it. Billy watched his receding figure, trying not to feel abandoned.

As soon as his father was out of sight, he began to explore. There was a tiny yard, with no swings or anything. How different this was from his school in Bath, with its broad playing fields and troops of boys in blue blazers and caps. This strange new place would take some getting used to, the little school and the house without a garden.

'Daddy said we'd be late,' said Sarah, 'and there's nobody here. Can we go home?'

'Of course not. The teacher will be here soon.'

'Why is she called Miss Shute?'

'That's her name.'

'But why? It's a silly name.'

The door opened behind her, and a voice said, 'You must be the Palmer children.'

She was spare and pale, her greying hair tied in a bun, a plain black dress flapping around her ankles. They followed her through

3

a hallway and into a classroom. It was very bare, containing only desks for twelve children, a table and a chair. Sitting beneath the blackboard was another woman dressed in black. She rose heavily as they entered.

'This is Miss Shute,' said Miss Shute.

Where the first was spare, the second was stout. They were different renderings of the same idea: even the features of their faces were the same; but one was all angles and the other all curves. Their wintry blue eyes rested on Billy and Sarah.

'We hope you will be happy here,' said the first Miss Shute. 'Where did you go to school before?'

'I went to the Unicorn School,' said Billy.

'And I went to St Mary's,' said Sarah.

'And what were your best subjects?'

'Reading and writing,' said Billy unhesitatingly.

'I don't know,' said Sarah. 'I liked them all.'

'Well, that's good.'

'I don't think I will be happy here,' said Sarah.

'Why do you say that, my child?' said the second Miss Shute.

'I don't think I like you.'

The Misses Shute looked at one another and sighed. 'I think you will grow to like us,' said the second. 'We may seem stern to you, but we're not really.'

'Billy, what did you read last at the Unicorn School?' said the first Miss Shute.

'*Treasure Island*, miss.'

'Did you like it?'

'Yes, a lot.'

'Then for your first lesson this morning you will write about your favourite character in *Treasure Island*. Who is that?'

'Jim Hawkins.'

'Very good. And what have you been reading, Sarah?'

'*The Water-Babies*,' said Sarah, shy now.

'And who do you like in *The Water-Babies*?'

Sarah considered for a moment and glanced at her brother for encouragement. 'Well . . . I *quite* like Ellie. But the one I really like is Mrs Doasyouwouldbedoneby.'

'Then your first task will be to copy out some pages about Mrs Doasyouwouldbedoneby and Mrs Bedonebyasyoudid. Is your handwriting neat?'

'No.'

'Yes it is, Sarah,' said Billy. 'Mum's helped you with it.'

'No it isn't,' she insisted. 'It's . . . straggly.'

'We'll soon see,' said the first Miss Shute. 'Miss Shute will be your teacher, Sarah, and Billy, I will be yours. Assembly is in this

5

classroom. I would like you both to stand at the front so that I may introduce you.'

There was a commotion in the hallway, and two boys burst into the classroom. The first was very tall, a little older than Billy, and the second was about Sarah's age. They were both lean and bony, with shocks of ginger hair and large ears. Billy wondered whether everyone here came in twos.

'This is Frank and Ed Willmott,' said the first Miss Shute. Frank, the elder, looked Billy up and down before going to a desk at the back of the classroom. More children began to arrive.

'Why are there two Miss Shutes?' said Sarah to Billy.

'One for your class and one for mine.'

'Are they sisters?'

'They must be.'

'I think they're creepy.'

Twenty or so children filled the room. They whispered to one another and stole glances at Billy and Sarah. There was an air of informality that Billy was quite unused to. The boy who stood next to him was about his age. He had freckles and a sly smile, and repeatedly looked sidelong at him without saying anything. Miss Shute asked the children to close their eyes and say the Lord's Prayer. Billy sensed the other boy leaning

6

towards him as he began. 'Our Father, who farts in heaven . . . ' He opened his eyes and looked at the boy, whose face wore an expression of complicity. ' . . . lead us not into detention, but deliver us from teacher. Amen.'

'We have two new children in the school today,' said Miss Shute. 'Billy and Sarah Palmer have come from Bath. We know you will make them feel at home here.'

The younger children, including Sarah and Ed, went to the second classroom, leaving four boys and six girls. 'Billy, please sit next to Alan,' said Miss Shute. The desks were constructed in pairs, with sloping tops, empty inkwells and pencils lying in grooves. Miss Shute gave Billy some paper. 'Alan, will you look after Billy?' she said to the freckled boy. 'I hope you will be friends.'

'Yes, miss,' said Alan. 'He looks all right.' And to Billy, 'You look all right, I reckon.'

He began composing his essay. 'I like Jim Hawkins best of all the people in *Treasure Island* because he is very brave,' he wrote. 'Also, he has the same name as my Dad.'

Miss Shute moved around the room, speaking to them one at a time. With ten children ranging in age between eight and eleven there was no single set of lessons: each child was given something different to do.

Billy shaded his eyes and looked over at Alan's piece of paper. His handwriting was rambling and effortful. 'Henry the Aith had six wives,' Billy read. 'They were not very good wives so he chopped of there heads.'

He looked around the room. The other children were talking freely, and not much work was getting done. Behind him, Frank Willmott and another boy were squabbling over possession of a rubber. Billy looked up at Miss Shute, who seemed quite unconcerned. After an hour or so she asked the children to stop what they were doing, and began reading from *Lorna Doone*. 'This is a good story,' whispered Alan. 'The Doones are a very bad lot, going around murdering people. But John Ridd'll take care of 'em.'

At morning break the children dashed into the yard, the boys and the girls occupying their separate territories. Frank Willmott laid a hand on Billy's shoulder and said, 'So, Billy Palmer, you have to run the gauntlet.'

'What's that?'

'It's what you have to do to be a member of the school. Come on, lads, let's show him.'

The other boys stood with their hands flat against the classroom wall.

'You go through four times,' said Frank. 'The first time you get rain, the second time you get lightning, the third time you get thunder, and the fourth time you get hailstones.' He took up a position at the other end. 'Now, run!'

Billy ducked and entered the tunnel created by the boys' arms. As he did so the first boy, Ed, slapped him on the back. Each in turn gave him a slap, the last and hardest being Frank's. 'Now, back to the front,' he said. Billy ran again, this time being rabbit-punched; the third time it was prods with the knee. He was soon hurting a lot, and tears were starting in his eyes. Frank's final blow, a punch in the stomach, was vicious. He was very strong, despite being so wiry, and he seemed to be enjoying himself.

The gauntlet broke up, and Billy tried to face Frank down. Tears were welling in his eyes, but he knew he mustn't wipe them away. He set his mouth firm.

'You are now a member of the school,' said Frank. 'But you have to tell us some things about yourself.'

'All right.'

'So you're from Bath. Why have you come here?'

'Because my dad's got a new job.'

'What's that, then?'

'It's in an outfitters in Wells. Selling clothes.'

'And what did he do before?'

'He sold cars.'

'What sort of cars?'

'Jaguars.'

Billy sensed a change in the attitude of the boys. This part of his initiation had suddenly become interesting.

'Your dad sold Jaguars?' said Frank.

'Yes,' said Billy. 'We had one too, a Mark Eight.'

'You mean you got to ride in a Mark Eight?' said Alan wonderingly.

'Yes. All the time.'

Frank considered this information for a moment. 'I think you're a liar,' he said, and the mood of the boys changed again.

'No I'm not,' said Billy. 'Ask my sister, she'll tell you.'

'Why hasn't he got his fancy Jaguar now, then?'

'I don't know,' said Billy. His father had never really explained.

'I think you're a liar, Billy Palmer. Liar, liar, pants on fire.'

'No I'm not!' shouted Billy. Why didn't he believe him? Of course they'd had a Jaguar. It was the best car of all.

'Cross your heart and hope to die.'

'Cross my heart and hope to die.'

'Well do it, then,' said Frank, a glint of menace in his eyes. 'Cross your heart.'

Billy did as he was told, while Frank looked at him sceptically. 'I'll get my sister to talk to yours,' he said. 'And if you're lying, you're for it.'

'I'm not. Sarah will tell you. She always wanted to sit in the front, but Dad wouldn't let her.'

Miss Shute appeared in the doorway and called the children back in. As they were crossing the yard Alan said to Billy in a low tone, 'I believe you. What colour was it?'

'Indigo blue.'

Alan whistled softly. 'Indigo blue,' he said with a faraway smile.

★　★　★

Jim cycled past the church hall and the village shop and out onto the Launcherley road. This journey of four miles into Wells would now be his daily lot, his daily penance, so different from the ten-minute drive to the showroom in Bath. The road skirted the hills, passing through flat farmland. It was harvest time. Never having thought very much about the countryside, he must now learn to understand it. He wondered how the kids were getting on. This school seemed hardly a school at all, more a place to leave children during the day. And those spinster sisters were very odd. Well, Billy and Sarah would have to make do, just as he would have to.

He cycled past apple orchards and open fields. A wood pigeon flew from a tangled hedge, startling him for a moment. He saw a large farm up ahead, and smelled the sweet, raw odour of silage. Then at a crest in the road the façade of Wells Cathedral came into sight. He had come here once with Margaret, just before they were married, to visit her Uncle Reg and his wife. It was really a market town, he thought, not a city; the great edifice at its centre gave it airs.

Reg's shop was in Market Place. Jim dismounted and pushed his bicycle along the cobbled street. At one end was a stone cross with a fountain, and at the other the Bishop's Eye, the gateway to the palace. This stately tranquillity made him uneasy.

A sign etched in gold above one of the shops read 'Underhill's', and below, 'Outfitters to the Scholars & Gentry of Wells'. The windows curved inwards towards a recessed door, and displayed school uniforms and dull men's clothes. Jim pushed his bike into a narrow, gloomy space.

'You can park it out the back,' said Reg, barely looking up as he spoke. Catching sight of himself in a mirror, Jim hastily removed his bicycle clips. In his tweed jacket and grey flannels he was hot and flustered after his ride. He swept back his wavy brown hair and took another look at himself, at the new assistant in Underhill's Outfitters.

'It'll be slow for a week or two,' said Reg. 'You've missed the back-to-school rush, for which you should be very grateful. And nobody's thinking about winter just yet. I need to do stocktaking and accounts, so I'm going to leave the customers to you.'

Reg was a small, fastidious man, his grey hair crinkly and glistening with Brylcreem. His eyes are too close together, thought Jim, squint eyes.

'Are the prices on everything?'

'There's a list,' said Reg, reaching into a drawer under the till. 'Here. Now, I don't want you trying to sell anything to anybody, understand? This isn't like what you're used to. If somebody wants something they'll buy it.'

Jim was good at selling. The last thing he'd sold was an XK150 Drophead. He had persuaded the buyer to take just about every extra going, from the Dunlop racing tyres to the wood-rim steering wheel. If Reg didn't want Jim to sell, then more fool him.

Reg went into the office at the back, leaving him alone in the shop. He looked at the price list, and tried to relate it to what was on display. Everything seemed to come in a shade of grey or brown — there was nothing remotely fashionable, no modern fabrics or bright colours. The dark wood of the fixtures oppressed him, and he stood at the front of the shop gazing out into the street, at the few people who passed by. Perhaps Mondays were always quiet, he thought. It was ages before the doorbell rang.

'I want a cap,' said his first customer. He was florid and thickset, a clod of a man.

'Yes, sir,' said Jim. 'What sort of cap?'

'One like this,' the man said, removing a worn flat cap from his head. He examined it through thick glasses, turning it over in his hands. 'Had this one twenty years.'

'What size is it?'

'Blowed if I know. The label went a long time ago.'

Jim went over to the display of caps. 'Try this,' he said, choosing the plainest. The man tried it on in front of the mirror.

'How much?'

Jim returned to the counter and the list. 'Seven and six,' he said.

'Got anything cheaper?'

Jim handed him another, almost identical cap.

'This one's six shillings.'

The man tried it on. 'I can't see any

14

difference,' he said.

Jim took the caps back. He couldn't see any difference either. 'This one has a better quality lining,' he said involuntarily. 'It'll last longer.'

The man took them back and looked at the linings. 'I think you're right,' he said. 'I'll take it.'

At lunchtime Jim stepped out into the sunshine, breathing in the warm air with a sense of grateful relief. He walked through Penniless Porch, the towered archway that separated the town from the cathedral precincts, and onto the green. Sitting down on the grass he slowly ate his sandwiches, and then lay back and closed his eyes. He'd had one customer that morning, and had taken a trifling sum of money. Wondering how he was going to get through the afternoon, he drifted into sleep.

When he awoke it was to a thrilling, reverberant sound. The bells of the cathedral were ringing. But this was no ordinary bell-ringing: it was an intricate music, full of complex harmonies. It seemed to go on forever, oceanic, washing over him. When it ended he sat up, collected his things, and began to walk slowly back to the shop. He felt utterly stranded.

★   ★   ★

Margaret tidied the breakfast table and riddled the ashes in the stove. She wasn't sure whether she was daunted more by the prospect of her tasks or by the time stretching ahead of her. Certainly there would be many more chores than she had lately been used to. But then there would be little else. Hubert Fosse had lived in this cottage until his wife died, when he moved into an outbuilding at the back. The furniture consisted of the few sticks they had been allowed to hold onto, and things that Fosse had left behind. Margaret's sole indulgence was the Roberts radio she had hidden in the airing cupboard the day the receiver came to do the inventory. The *Light Programme* would be her society now.

She went out into the yard behind the house. Margaret had had a single brief conversation with Fosse since they moved in two days ago, and she felt she should try to get to know him. His farm was a small one, with twenty-odd Friesian cows, two pigs, and some chickens and geese. He was in the milking shed, washing down the stalls, and he stood awkwardly as Margaret entered, stretching his back. Margaret thought he was the ruddiest man she had ever seen. His bald

16

head was peeling from the sun, and his white hair seemed to come from everywhere except the top of his head — from his ears, his nose, and, most dramatically, from his chest, overflowing the collar of his shirt. It was like a pelt.

'Good morning, Hubert,' said Margaret.

'Morning.'

'I was wondering whether I could be of any help to you.'

'You'll have enough to do, I guess, with your family.'

'Yes, I'm sure. But there'll be times, I expect. Did Uncle Reg tell you I was a land girl during the war?'

'No, he didn't.' He emptied a bucket of water across the floor and picked up a broom.

'It's a long time ago now, of course. But I know something about dairy farming. And I used to be able to milk.'

'Well, I could surely use a hand with the milking. But that means getting up at six.'

'I'm up at six these days anyway.'

'Then put your head around the shed door any morning,' he said, beginning to scrub. 'I can't pay you, though. All I can do is give you some milk.'

'That would be most welcome.'

Margaret sensed that the conversation was at an end. But as she turned to go, Hubert said, 'Maybe there are things I can do for you too. It must be hard, all this.'

'Thank you.' She looked away from him. 'Yes, it is hard. But much harder for Jim.' She wanted to go on, wanted to talk of the shame Jim felt over losing his business. She realized that she wanted to talk to someone very much. Instead, she simply wished Fosse good morning and stepped back into the yard. She stood for a moment gazing at the cottage. It was an odd sort of place, its roofs steeply gabled, the windows hung with white shutters. It's a gingerbread house, she thought. Well, it could be much worse. She entered the kitchen and opened the door of the larder. The shelves seemed very empty, and this reminder that she must replenish them came to her as a surprise.

Crossing the bridge by the school she looked out for Billy and Sarah, but they were in class. The village shop bore a sign that read 'Lyons Tea — The Tea of Teashop Fame'. She thought back to the tea-rooms in Bath, to lazy mornings spent nursing a cup of coffee and gossiping with her friends. The moment she entered, the tiny woman behind the counter said, 'Mrs Palmer, if I may guess. Welcome to the village.'

'Thank you.'

'We don't get many strangers here. Not

that you're a stranger, of course. Bath is where you're coming from, now, isn't it?'

'That's right.'

'You'll find things a little slower here.'

Margaret looked around the shop, its shelves stacked high with groceries.

'I don't think I'll mind that,' she said.

'Good. Now what can I get you?'

Margaret hadn't really discussed house-keeping with Jim. It was one of the subjects that seemed difficult to broach at the moment. She would just have to see how much things cost.

'Do you have meat?' she asked.

'You get that from the butcher's van. You just have to flag him down one day and make an arrangement.' Margaret imagined herself roaming the lanes in search of a butcher. 'Capstone's his name. Come here tomorrow about eleven and I'll see if I can find him for you.'

She spent the rest of the morning doing the washing, and in the afternoon she fell asleep. When she awoke, for a moment she imagined herself to be in the airy bedroom at the big house in Bath. She had often slept in the afternoon there, but more from boredom than from the weariness she felt now. The children would be home from school soon. But first she would steal an hour at Mansfield

Park. Henry Crawford had just proposed to Fanny Price, and Fanny had foolishly accepted.

Billy appeared a couple of minutes before Sarah. For a while he had tried to keep pace with her, but in the end he had given up and run on. He was halfway up the stairs when Margaret called him back.

'You must wait for your sister,' she said, 'and take care of her.'

'But she's so *slow*.'

'She's seven, Billy, and she shouldn't have to find her own way home.'

Sarah opened the door as Margaret was speaking. 'I can find my own way home,' she said. 'It's easy.'

'How was your first day at school?'

'It was horrible,' said Sarah. 'The Miss Shutes are *witches*.'

'No they're not,' said Billy, 'they're just old.'

'Yes they are. I saw their broom.'

'No you didn't.'

'I did,' said Sarah emphatically. 'It was in a cupboard.'

'Perhaps they use it for sweeping the floor,' said Margaret.

'It's a special flying broom.'

'You know there are good witches as well as wicked ones, don't you?'

Sarah looked at her mother with a grave expression. 'The Miss Shutes are *very* wicked,' she said.

Jim got home at six, and they sat down to eat. After supper Billy and Sarah went exploring in the farmyard.

'How did it go?' Margaret asked Jim.

'It was awful, Maggie,' he said. 'I'm not sure how I'm going to do this. Reg obviously dislikes me, for a start.'

'I'm sure he doesn't. He gave you a job, remember, when no one else would.'

'Yes, and he's going to lose no opportunity to remind me of that.'

Margaret sat down and kissed him on the cheek. 'Then you must gain his respect,' she said.

'And how do I do that?'

'I don't know . . . by doing a good job.'

'He more or less told me he doesn't *want* me to do a good job. A child could do it.'

He slumped into the armchair and picked up the newspaper, turning to the cartoons. Margaret stood and began to clear away the supper things. What will he do in the evenings? she wondered. The children would find things, and she would read. But Jim had spent his with the television and the record player. What was he going to do without Sergeant Bilko and Artie Shaw?

21

It was difficult to get Billy and Sarah to bed: it was still light, and they sensed that with their new surroundings should come new routines, new privileges. But it was barely ten by the time Jim went upstairs. Margaret read for a while longer before following him, and spent a long time in the bathroom. There was no mirror save for Jim's shaving mirror, and she was glad of that. In recent years she had become aware of changes in herself, of the ways in which her body had been betrayed by age and the children. She combed her hair slowly and splashed water over her face. Jim lay on his back in the half-light, gazing at the ceiling, and when she got in beside him she waited tensely for a moment. And as he had done every night for a long time now, he leaned over, kissed her lightly, and turned his back.

★　★　★

By the end of Billy's first week at school, he and Alan were friends. One morning Alan came by the farmhouse, and they set off across the fields. Billy hadn't been sure where he was able to go, but Alan wandered freely, so he simply followed. They walked through an apple orchard, and Alan told him that scrumping time would come soon.

'What's scrumping?'

'Stealing apples.'

'Is it allowed?' said Billy, feeling immediately foolish.

' 'Course it isn't. That's the point. We'll do it with Frank and the rest of the gang. He'll tell us when.'

They crossed a stile and came into the field where Fosse's cows were pastured.

'Will they chase us?' said Billy.

'Watch.'

Alan began to run straight at them. They scattered before him, and he ran back to Billy with an exultant expression on his face. 'See,' he said. 'Scaredy cows.'

At the top of Folly Lane there was a birch copse. Alan led the way to a place at the edge from where they could see the countryside stretching before them. It was criss-crossed by ditches that ran very straight alongside tracks and hedges.

'Are they canals?' said Billy.

'They're called rhynes.'

'Rinds?'

'No, *rhynes*. R-h-y-n-e-s.'

Glastonbury Tor dominated everything, a pyramid on the plain.

'So what do you know about the tor?' said Billy.

'It's where King Arthur's buried, isn't it?'

'King Arthur of the Round Table?'

'Yes.'

'I thought he lived in Camelot.'

'But he died here. Avalon, they called it.'

Billy's eyes returned to the tor. 'Have you been there?' he said.

'My dad took me in the milk lorry once. You can see for miles.'

'Do you think your dad would take *me* there?'

'Maybe.'

They lapsed into silence for a moment. Alan sucked on a blade of grass and said, 'My dad says all this used to be under the sea, and Avalon was an island.'

'You mean when he was a kid?'

'No, a long time ago. Hundreds of years, maybe thousands.'

Billy gazed at the plain. How exciting, he thought, that all this might once have been under water. They would have needed a boat to get to school. But then the school would have been under water too. It was hard sometimes to account for things, for how strange the world seemed. He narrowed his eyes. 'Alan,' he said. 'You know when you see colours, like green and blue . . . do you think everybody sees the same thing?'

'How do you mean?'

'Well, how do I know that what I see as

green you don't see as blue?'

Alan thought for a moment. 'We've got the same eyes, haven't we?'

Billy looked at him, then back towards the tor. It held his attention all the time. 'Come on,' he said suddenly. 'Race you back down the hill.'

★ ★ ★

At the weekend the cottage was eerily quiet. Billy was soon bored, and tried without success to interest first his sister and then his mother in playing games. His father ignored him, reading the newspaper from cover to cover and back again. Then just as Billy was giving up on him, he said, 'Let's do the British Grand Prix, shall we?'

'All right.'

They got out the Dinky toy set and the scale model of Aintree race-track that his father had helped Billy to construct a year or so before. Billy's Dinky toy cars had been his prize possession. Jim had bought him any number of them, including gift sets such as the racing cars and the sports cars. And since they had gone together to the British Grand Prix the previous summer, they had often re-enacted that marvellous day. The Jaguar people had given Jim passes for the paddock and the pits, and before the race they had been able to stroll about among the cars and meet the drivers, those nonchalant heroes in their white overalls and armoured helmets. Every moment of that day was seared on Billy's memory: the deafening noise, the acrid smell of petrol, the sheer exhilaration of it all.

They set up the track, placing the pits and the grandstands and the barriers in the right places.

'Who's in pole position?' said Jim.

'Stirling Moss,' said Billy, as he always did. 'With Mike Hawthorn beside him. Then Fangio and Brooks, and Collins at the back.' There were only five cars in the set, but these had always been enough to create the atmosphere they wanted. Jim waved a tiny flag, and Billy moved forward Moss's Vanwall and Hawthorn's Ferrari. At the first bend Hawthorn tried to edge past, but Moss turned sharply and entered the straight in front. Jim brought Fangio's Maserati and Brooks's Vanwall up behind; Collins would be relegated to last place throughout.

They completed two laps. 'We forgot the fire engine,' said Jim. But Billy went on, manoeuvring the cars one by one through bends and chicanes and down fast straights. He decided he would make things more interesting by having Fangio overtake Brooks and make ground on Moss and Hawthorn: this race wasn't coming alive as it used to. Then suddenly he crashed Moss's Vanwall into a barrier, flipping it over onto the floor. He sat for a moment surveying the havoc he had wrought.

'Dad,' he said, 'this isn't very exciting any more, is it?'

'Why not?'

'I don't know. It's not . . . real.'

'But we're remembering it, like it was at Aintree.'

Billy stood up. 'I think this is for kids,' he said. He looked at his father with an expression that mixed apology and defiance. And then he ran out of the door into the yard.

★　★　★

Margaret got up at six and went quietly downstairs to the kitchen. She put on her oldest pair of slacks and one of Jim's jerseys, and tied her hair in a scarf. Hubert was leading the cows into the milking shed. 'You'll need wellingtons,' he said. 'I'll get my wife's.'

In the dark of the shed the cows loomed large and strange. She hadn't been near one for many years. They bellowed in their stalls, and shifted their feet uneasily. They want this over with, she thought, want to be rid of their load. She ran her hand down the coarse black hair of the nearest. They were so ponderous, and so docile. Hubert gave her a pair of wellingtons. 'The pail and stool are over there,' he said. 'You'll need a cup for the foremilk.'

Margaret placed the stool close to the haunches of the cow; its udder was swollen, and marbled with thick veins. She began tentatively, drawing a little milk from each teat into the cup, and then she placed the pail in its place and began to work. After a while she found her rhythm, and the cow became still, pacified by her touch. The milk seethed as it struck the metal. When the pail was full she took it over to the cooling machine and poured the milk into the reservoir at the top, watching it trickle over the iron corrugations and into the churn below.

When they were finished Hubert gave her a jug of milk, and she carried it out into the yard. On the way to the kitchen door she stopped to look at the pigs, Stan and Gertie. Gertie gave her a penetrating stare. They were revolting creatures, and yet there was something rather likeable about them.

Jim and Billy and Sarah were up by now.

'Look, warm milk,' said Sarah.

'It's not pasteurised,' said Jim.

'And nor was the milk you and I grew up on.'

'It tastes funny,' said Billy.

'Just drink it,' said Margaret. 'It'll do you good.'

★ ★ ★

The weather was changing as Jim set off for Wells, and by the time he arrived at the shop it was starting to rain. Towards the end of the previous week trade had picked up, but this Monday was as slow as his first, the pall lifted only by the arrival of a delivery from Askews in Bristol. Reg spent the morning checking the clothes against the despatch note, fussing over discrepancies. He was getting on Jim's nerves. Whenever Jim offered to do anything more than stand behind the counter and deal with customers he dismissed him, saying that it would take longer to explain than to do it himself. Jim's predecessor had been nineteen. If Reg had given him this job solely out of charity, then they would both have to accept the pretences that came with it.

He ate his sandwiches in the stockroom and listened to the rain. He must get out for a while. He hadn't brought a raincoat, so he turned up the collar of his jacket and thrust his hands in his pockets. A little way down

Sadler Street was Goody's café, and he ducked through the door and into an airless room. Condensation ran down the windows, obscuring the world outside. He sat at a table in the corner and lit up a smoke, while a middle-aged woman bustled behind the counter. The menu tacked to the wall offered sausage, egg and chips and baked beans on toast. Jim would gladly have given his sandwiches a miss and eaten lunch here, but with what? The seven pounds a week from Underhill's would be stretched as it was.

A girl appeared through the door at the back, and came over to take his order. Jim hadn't set eyes on a young woman since he came to Wells: he seemed to come across only old people and children. Girls must be somewhere, he'd presumed. Well, here was one. He sat up a little straighter, all his senses suddenly alert.

'A cup of tea, please,' he said.

She smiled and turned back to the counter. There was something open and direct in her manner that Jim found appealing. And she had a gorgeous figure, with slim hips and full breasts that her apron couldn't hide. She returned with Jim's cup of tea. 'Anything else?' she said. Jim knew from the way she hesitated that she returned his interest. She had long dark hair that hadn't been permed or fooled about with, and her lipstick wasn't overdone. Her brown eyes drew Jim in. 'No thanks, love,' he said.

She began wiping down the other tables, and Jim made a show of looking away from her; but with the windows steamed up there wasn't really anywhere else to direct his gaze. He sipped his tea and dragged on his cigarette, wondering how best to arrange his arms and legs.

Jim attracted women, and he knew it. He'd never had any trouble. Well, the trouble had always been that there *was* no trouble. He'd strayed many times since he got married. It was easy when you had money and a car and reasons to be out in the evenings. The last one had been a receptionist at the showroom. That had got messy, and after she left, Jim swore he would stay faithful to Margaret. But that was a year ago now, and since then everything had changed.

★   ★   ★

Billy was settling into a routine at school. Miss Shute took a particular interest in him, and encouraged his reading. She seemed little concerned with other subjects, and this suited him very well. Books, and with them history,

31

were what she cared about. Billy had been biding his time for a few days now, waiting for his moment.

'Miss, I'd like to know about Glastonbury Tor,' he said. 'And King Arthur.'

'A very good idea, Billy. Have you read about King Arthur?'

'No. I know he had a round table, and some knights. And Alan says he's buried in the tor.'

Miss Shute glanced across at Alan. 'Not in the tor, in the abbey.' She looked at Billy for a moment. 'I have just the book for you,' she said. She stepped into the tiny storeroom and returned with a sturdy, greenbound volume. *King Arthur and His Knights of the Round Table*, he read, by Roger Lancelyn Green. 'This will be your next book,' said Miss Shute. 'You must read about Arthur, and Lancelot and Guinevere, and Sir Gawain and the Green Knight, and Sir Galahad and the Holy Grail. This is our heritage, Billy. Do you know what that means?'

'No, miss.'

'It means our past, our history. These are the first stories of Britain. They're wonderful stories, too.'

Billy leafed through the book, gazing at the woodcut illustrations of these magnificent characters. The first chapter was called 'The

Two Swords'. He began reading straight away.

At morning break the boys played 'it', racing around the little playground. No matter how hard Billy tried to tag Frank Willmott, his long skinny arm would reach out and tag him straight back. Frank's brother Ed came off worst. 'Titch', they called him, though he wasn't much smaller than Billy and Alan. When they stopped for a breather, Frank gave Billy one of his calculating looks.

'You're a swot,' he said.

'No I'm not.'

'And a crawler,' said Les Vowles, who seldom spoke except to echo Frank.

'You've always got your nose in a book.'

'So?'

'So . . . you're a swot.' Frank paused for a moment. 'What's that book, then, about King Arthur?'

'Well, it's about King Arthur. And his knights.'

'What happens?'

'I've only just started it. Arthur is brought up by Merlin, who's a wizard. Then he pulls a sword out of a stone, and that means he's going to be King of Britain.'

'Just for pulling a sword out of a stone?'

'It's a special sword. It's called Excalibur.

And nobody else can pull it out.'

The other boys listened attentively to Billy. He had the sense that he was besting Frank, outwitting him. Who wouldn't want to read these stories of knights and swords and wizards and monsters? Frank looked at each of them in turn. 'Sounds like stuff and nonsense to me,' he said.

'Well it isn't,' said Billy. 'It's good.'

Frank suddenly turned on Les and punched him hard on the arm.

'Ow! What did you do that for?'

'Let's do the Davy Crockett song,' he said. He turned back to Billy. 'I bet you don't know the Davy Crockett song.'

'No.'

Frank smiled archly. 'Come on, lads,' he said, and with that the four boys began to sing:

'Born on a mountaintop in Tennessee,
Killed his ma when he was only three,
Killed his pa when he was only four,
And now he's looking for his brother-
    in-law.
Davy, Davy Crockett, king of the wild
    frontier.'

Eager to repeat the joke, they immediately began the verse again. Frank sang lustily, apparently sure of his renewed authority. Billy picked up the words and sang along too. As they filed back into the school, a truce seemed to have been called.

Billy and Sarah walked home at the end of the day, or rather, Sarah walked and Billy ran back and forth and in circles around her. They passed a house that was called Tanyard Cottage.

'Miss Vale lives there,' said Sarah. 'Trish says she's got a hundred cats.'

'A hundred? No she doesn't.'

'She does too.'

'Nobody has a hundred cats.' Billy leaned over the wall and looked into the weedy, overgrown garden. 'Where are they, then?' he said.

'They're all inside,' said Sarah, straining to see. 'She doesn't let them out, in case people steal them.'

Billy could see no sign of any cats. 'Let's ask Mum,' he said, and with that he ran off. For once Sarah followed, and they were both out of breath by the time they got home.

'Does Miss Vale have a hundred cats?' Sarah asked Margaret the moment they came into the kitchen.

'Who is Miss Vale?'

'She's got a hundred cats.'

'*Where* has she got a hundred cats?'

'She lives at Tanyard Cottage, Mum,' said Billy. 'You know, the tumbledown place on the road to school.'

Margaret looked from one to the other for a moment. 'Well, there's only one way to find out how many cats she's got. We'd best pay her a visit.'

'Oh, when?' said Sarah.

'On Saturday morning,' said Margaret decisively. 'It's about time we got to know our neighbours.'

★　★　★

On the way to Tanyard Cottage, Billy climbed the first gate, as he always did now, to take in the view of the tor. A curtain of rain was sweeping across the countryside, the sun breaking, through here and there like the beams of a car's headlamps. They had to race to the cottage so as not to get caught in a shower.

They knocked on the door and waited, and after a few moments heard a voice call out 'Coming'.

She seemed to Billy to be old but somehow not old. She had a nest of red hair and piercing green eyes, and her face was caked with white powder. Her dress, a blue smock, was wrinkled and dirty.

'Hello, poppets,' she said.

'Miss Vale?' said Margaret.

'Yes.'

'My name's Margaret Palmer. We've just moved into Coombe.'

Miss Vale raised her hand distractedly and brushed her hair. 'Come in,' she said.

In the barely furnished sitting room Billy was almost overcome by the smell of pee. Did it come from Miss Vale, he wondered, or from the cats? Sarah looked about her, turning from one side to the other in search of any sign of them. Margaret laid her hands on Sarah's shoulders and set her straight.

'Would you like some tea?' said Miss Vale.

'That's very kind of you, but we've just had breakfast.'

They sat down.

'And where have you come from?'

'From Bath.'

'From Bath,' said Miss Vale pensively. 'I used to live in London. And lots of other places.' She paused, seeming to be about to say something more but then thinking better of it. Then she said, 'That was a long time ago, when I was a dancer.'

'You were a dancer?' said Sarah.

'I was a very *good* dancer.'

Billy sat staring at this colourful creature. In his experience old ladies were not dancers;

indeed they weren't anything at all, except old.

'Have you got a hundred cats?' said Sarah in a hushed voice.

'Well, I'm really not sure.' Miss Vale looked about her as if to consider where they might be hiding. 'Shall we count them?'

'Yes, please,' said Sarah.

'They're in the other room,' she said, and rose from the chair. The three of them followed her to the door, which she flung open as if to reveal wonders.

They were everywhere, Miss Vale's cats, on chairs, on tables, in baskets and on the floor. The older ones stared vacantly, while the young ones tumbled towards them. Sarah gasped in astonishment, picking up a tabby kitten, and Billy began counting, a judicious expression forming on his features. 'Thirty-one,' he said eventually. 'No, thirty-two. I think.' Miss Vale cooed at them, appearing not to mind that they were tearing her furniture apart and neglecting the litter trays.

'This one seems to have taken a fancy for you, poppet,' she said to Sarah. 'Would you like to have it?'

'Oh, yes! Can I, Mummy?'

'I'm not sure. We should ask your father first.'

'Please, Mummy. *Please.*'

Sarah cradled the kitten in her arms, and it purred its way to sleep.

'Very well. But if your father objects it must come straight back, do you understand?'

'He'll love it. Is it a girl or a boy?'

'I've really no idea,' said Miss Vale. 'It's one or the other.'

'I think it's a girl.'

Billy looked at his sister. He was sure he would end up looking after this kitten, just like the hamster Sarah had insisted on having the year before.

'We should be going now,' said Margaret. 'Perhaps we could call on you another time?'

★ ★ ★

Jim returned to Goody's a few days after his first visit. The girl was there again, and her smile of recognition was intoxicating.

'What's your name?' he said when she brought him his tea.

'Liz,' she replied. 'Liz Burridge.'

'I'm Jim Palmer.'

'I know you are,' she said, fidgeting with her apron strings.

'You do? How's that?'

'Oh, people talk. And you're new around here.'

'What do they say?'

She glanced across at the woman behind the counter, who was looking at her disapprovingly. 'Perhaps I shouldn't say.'

'Well, you have to now, don't you?' he said, teasing her. 'What time do you get off work?'

'Half past five.'

'Me too. How about a drink in the Star?'

An expression of alarm crossed her face. 'Tonight?' she said.

'Why not?'

'I don't think I can.'

'Where's the harm in it?'

'I . . . I've got to cook supper for my mum and dad.'

'Another day, then.'

'I don't know. Perhaps.'

He paid for his cup of tea and stepped back out into the rain. Moody and irritable, he took up his position behind the counter in the shop. There was nothing for him nowadays, nothing to enjoy, nothing to look forward to.

Over the course of the next few days he found that his thoughts kept on returning to Liz Burridge, and on another damp morning he returned to Goody's determined to try again.

'How about tonight?' he said abruptly as she approached his table.

She tugged at her apron strings and looked

40

out of the window. 'All right,' she said after a few moments.

He looked up at her in surprise. 'See you in the Star, then,' he said. 'Half past five.'

'Yes.'

She turned away, and Jim reached into his pocket for some change. He had less than he'd thought. Back in the shop, he spent the afternoon in a state of agitation. How was he going to explain his being late to Margaret? Supper would be on the table by six as usual. Well, he'd have to make something up. A boy from the Cathedral School came in and bought a couple of pairs of socks. Somehow the two shillings ended up in Jim's pocket, and he left the sale off the sheet. He was instantly dismayed by what he had done, but at the same time incapable of undoing it.

After Reg closed up the shop, Jim wheeled his bike to the Star Hotel and found an empty table away from the other drinkers. A blue smoke haze hung in the air, lit up by the last rays of the sun. The Star was where the commercial travellers went, and those farmers who could afford to stay on after market day and have a night away from their wives. There wasn't a woman in sight. When Liz arrived the drinkers stirred momentarily before lapsing back into their torpor. Jim ordered a pint of bitter and a cider.

'Cheers,' he said, and he levelled a candid look at her. There wasn't much she'd been able to do to her appearance since lunchtime, but clearly she had spent some time in front of a mirror. She seemed even prettier to him this evening.

'So what are these things people have been saying about me?' he said.

She smiled cagily, and smoothed down her black skirt. 'That you got into some sort of trouble. That you've come here to get away from it.'

'Is that so? And who exactly is saying these things?'

'That would be telling, wouldn't it?'

Jim took a draught of his beer and set down the glass. 'I'm a bankrupt, Liz, that's all. People don't seem to like bankrupts.'

'How did it happen?' Liz's expression had turned to one of concern.

'I was in the motor trade. I had the Jaguar franchise in Bath.'

'Classy,' she said.

'I had the Austin franchise before, but then I changed. And that's when things started to go wrong.'

'Why?'

'Oh, I don't know. Petrol rationing after Suez didn't help.'

She looked away for a moment, and then

back at him. 'This is a bit of a comedown, then,' she said softly.

'Reg Underhill's? You could say that.'

In the corner a foxy-looking man was reading the *Sporting Life* and glancing across at them. Jim gave him a challenging look, and he promptly buried his face in the paper. He turned his attention back to Liz.

'What about you?' he said. 'You're not planning to spend the rest of your days in Goody's, I hope.'

'I'm going to nursing school in Bristol in the spring,' she said. 'I've been filling in since I left school.'

Christ, he thought, how old is she? He'd imagined she was at least twenty, but he must be wrong.

'Did you grow up around here?'

'I was born here. My father runs the International Stores.'

'Like it?'

She shrugged. 'It's no good for people my age. There's nothing to do except go to the Regal on Saturdays. I'll be glad to get out.'

'What goes on at the Regal?'

'Oh, the matinees, you know. Westerns and that. And then sometimes there's music. That's the best. Lonnie Donegan came here in the summer.'

'You like Lonnie Donegan?'

'Not as much as Tommy Steele and Cliff Richard.'

'Big bands are what I like,' said Jim. He gazed down into his glass. 'Glenn Miller, Benny Goodman.'

'Eddie Calvert's coming soon, I think.'

He gave her a mocking smile. 'Eddie Calvert. 'Oh Mein Papa'. He's all right, I suppose.'

They fell silent for a while.

'I expect you're married,' said Liz, looking away and then back at him in that unnervingly direct way.

'You expect right. Does that bother you?'

'Not if it doesn't bother you,' she said.

He looked into her eyes, and she held his gaze.

'Would you like to go to the Eddie Calvert concert?' he said.

'Yes,' she replied. 'I would.'

2

At afternoon break, Frank gathered the older boys around him, with Ed tagging along as usual.

'It's scrumping time,' he said solemnly. 'Tomorrow morning, Alton's farm. Everybody in?'

The four of them nodded.

'Where's Alton's farm?' said Billy.

'It's on Southey Lane,' said Alan. 'I'll show you.'

The next morning Alan called by and they set off, heading in a direction that was new to Billy. There were apple orchards everywhere, the trees laden with red and green fruit.

'Do I need anything to carry the apples in?' he said.

'Just your pockets,' said Alan. 'It's not how many you can carry, it's just stealing them that's the fun.'

Frank and Ed and Les were already there, lounging against the wall of Alton's orchard. They climbed over and landed softly in the long grass among the windfall apples. 'The pigs like 'em,' said Ed, and he made a disgusting snuffling noise.

They broke up into two pairs, Frank and Ed and Billy and Alan, while Les was posted as guard. Under one of the smaller trees Ed straddled Frank's shoulders, and Frank raised himself to his full height. Ed began picking apples, first stuffing them into his pockets and then handing them down. Billy and Alan did the same, but Alan seemed very heavy on Billy's shoulders, and it wasn't long before they began to ache.

'I need a rest,' he said.

Alan clambered down. Their pockets were already bulging.

'Fagged so soon?' said Frank.

'Alan's heavier than Ed is,' said Billy.

'No he isn't. I'm just stronger than you, that's all.'

'Well, you're older.'

'Not by much.'

'Yeah,' said Les. 'Frank's stronger'n you. And he's not a crawler, either.'

Ed slipped from Frank's shoulders, and the boys stood in a circle. Frank was carelessly tossing an apple in his hand, and suddenly he drew back his arm and hurled it at Billy, striking him on the leg. Before Billy knew it, Alan had picked up an apple and thrown it at Frank, narrowly missing his head. As if by some unspoken command, the boys immediately retreated behind the nearest trees, Billy and Alan on one side and Frank, Ed and Les on the other, and began pelting one another with apples.

'This is *war!*' shouted Alan elatedly.

The boys darted out to collect more apples, and then dodged back behind the trees. With only two on their side, Billy and Alan were getting the worst of it. Just as they were beginning to run out, Billy saw a man appear at the gate.

'Oi! What the hell do you lot think you're doing!' he shouted.

The barrage ceased. Frank turned and ran, followed by Ed and Les. 'Let's go the other way,' said Alan, and he and Billy sprinted uphill towards the wood. Behind them they heard Frank and Les arguing about where to get over the wall.

'Frank Willmott,' said the farmer sharply. 'I might have known. Wait till your father hears about this.'

Billy and Alan soon made it to the middle of the wood. They stopped to catch their breath, and Alan started laughing uncontrollably. 'We won, Billy!' he said. 'We won the war!'

He took an apple from his pocket, rubbed it against his shorts, and took a big bite. Straight away he grimaced, and threw the apple into the trees.

'They're not ripe yet,' he said.

'What shall we do with them then?'

'Take 'em home and hide them for a bit.'

Billy had three apples in each of his pockets. He gave Alan two, and they set off for home. Four apples seemed a modest haul, and it didn't occur to Billy to conceal them further. When he appeared in the kitchen his father took one look at him and said, 'What have you been up to?'

'Exploring with Alan.'

'And what have you got in your pockets?'

Billy produced one of the apples.

'Alan's dad gave it to me.'

Jim looked at him sternly. 'Are you quite sure about that?' he said.

'Yes.'

Billy always hated telling lies, especially flimsy ones like this.

'I wouldn't want it thought that any son of mine went around stealing things.'

'No,' said Billy weakly, heading for the stairs.

'That's understood, then,' said his father. 'No stealing.'

'Yes, Dad.'

'And no telling tales.'

★   ★   ★

48

Margaret invited Reg Underhill and his wife Winifred to dinner, feeling that they owed them an expression of gratitude, both for giving Jim a job and for finding the cottage. She had never known them very well: her father and Reg were not close.

She bought a chicken from Hubert, which in consideration for her feelings he killed and beheaded. But the business of plucking and preparing it seemed to take all day. And then there was the wood stove to deal with: she had by now mastered it for boiling and frying, but grilling was a problem, and roasting an unknown. She packed the children off to bed early, despite their loud protestations, and at half past seven their guests arrived.

Reg was driving back and forth in his shiny black car in an attempt to find a place to park that wasn't muddy. As he got out he took a handkerchief from his pocket and wiped the bonnet.

'What do you think?' he said to Jim, standing back to admire it. 'New from Harris Motors.'

It was a Standard Vanguard. Jim knew it was a 1957 model, and that Reg's describing it as new was at the very least misleading.

'Very nice,' said Jim.

'Now *he*'s doing all right, is Harris.'

They sat around the kitchen table. Jim offered Reg a beer, and Winifred took in the cottage. Like her husband she was neat and sober in her appearance. And also like him, she was short and very broad in the beam.

'Well, this is cosy,' she said to Margaret.

'Oh, it's perfectly fine. We like it.' Margaret stooped to open the door of the stove, sure that the chicken was still quite raw. She pressed a fork into it, and pink juices flowed.

'How is Hubert these days?'

'It's hard to tell. He keeps himself to himself. But I'm helping him with the milking one or two days a week.'

'He needs to remarry,' said Reg. 'A man can't live without a woman, especially on a farm.'

'I don't think the marriage prospects are very good around here,' said Margaret. 'Especially for a man in his fifties.'

'And have you met any of your neighbours?' said Winifred.

'Just one, really, apart from people in the shop. A rather odd woman named Miss Vale.'

'Ah, Leonora Vale.' Winifred's eyes flashed mischievously. 'The scarlet woman of Coombe.'

'What do you know about her?'

'Well, she claims to have been in Isadora Duncan's dance school. Then I suppose

Isadora got tangled up in that scarf, and that was an end of it.'

'What do you mean she got tangled up in a scarf?' said Reg.

'She was wearing a long scarf and sitting in a sports car, and when it started off the scarf got caught in the back wheel and broke her neck.'

Margaret decided she really must get to know Leonora Vale.

'What about the Latymers?' said Winifred.

'The people in Coombe Hall, you mean?'

'Yes. But I suppose you're unlikely to set eyes on them.'

'Who are they?'

'He owns the Charlton Cider company in Shepton Mallet,' said Reg. 'Married to someone half his age who used to be a television announcer.'

'She's nothing like half his age,' said Winifred.

'She's a rich man's floozy, that's what she is.'

Winifred's eyes flashed again. 'You're just jealous, that's all,' she said, and turned to Margaret. 'Anyway, they stay behind those high walls of theirs, and I don't know anyone who's even so much as spoken to them.'

Margaret busied herself with dinner, willing the chicken to cook. Too soon Jim and

Reg had drunk all the beer, and there seemed little left to talk about. Margaret did what she could, but they remained stubbornly silent. She looked again at the chicken. A few hours earlier it had been strutting around the yard; now it seemed to be taking its revenge. Eventually she appealed to Winifred, who inspected it closely and suggested that it be quartered and fried. Jim carved it up and Margaret took out the largest pan. It was past nine by the time they ate.

Now and then Winifred cast her eyes across the table and made as if to speak, but then returned her attention to her plate. Eventually she said to Margaret, 'I expect you've been reading a lot. You always were a great reader.'

'I'm re-reading Jane Austen at the moment. I think I shall do that every few years from now on.'

'You know there's a mobile library, do you, that comes to the village once a month?'

'No, I didn't. Thank you for the tip.'

'On the subject of books,' said Reg, suddenly rousing himself, 'did you hear about the break-in at old man Pettigrew's?'

'You mean Pettigrew the printer?' said Jim.

'Yes. Has a big house out on Bristol Hill. The place was broken into the other night, and all they stole were his old books.'

'They were more than just old books, dear,'

said Winifred. 'They were antique books, and Alf Pettigrew's pride and joy.'

'They were probably very valuable,' said Margaret. 'Even my Everyman editions of Austen are worth something these days.'

'Time was you never heard about robberies and that sort of thing in Wells,' said Reg. 'I don't know what we're coming to.'

'Oh, don't be silly,' said Winifred. 'Wells is as quiet as the grave.'

Reg hacked at his chicken crossly. 'It may be for you, Winnie,' he said, 'but you don't have to put up with the school-kids and the Teddy boys. It's bloody mayhem at times, I can tell you.'

Winifred ignored her husband, and turned to Margaret. 'There's an amateur theatrical society I make costumes for,' she said. 'We're putting on Noël Coward's *Private Lives* in March, and you'd be perfect for the part of Amanda. Would you like to come to the auditions?'

'That would be rather difficult,' said Margaret, 'with the children and everything.'

'Yes, dear, of course.'

'But thank you for asking.'

The evening drew on. After a while even Winifred turned in on herself. She doesn't want to risk saying the wrong thing, thought Margaret, and it's so easy to say the wrong thing when things are so wrong in themselves.

Listening to the car drive away, Margaret realized she was exhausted. She started to clear the table, and suddenly burst into tears. Jim put his arms around her and stroked her hair. 'It's all right, Maggie,' he said. 'It's over now.'

★   ★   ★

Jim had been back to Goody's once, but it was awkward, and he decided he'd better find somewhere else to sit at lunchtime. The Eddie Calvert concert was still a week away, and he fought his impatience for it. Liz was occupying his thoughts to an alarming extent.

He walked up the High Street one day to the Star and settled into a chair with a pint of beer and the *Daily Express*. After a while the foxy-looking man he remembered from his evening with Liz entered and sat a few feet away. He began to read his *Sporting Life*, but then he folded it ostentatiously, as if trying to attract Jim's attention. Jim looked over, and the man nodded at him. Jim nodded back, but returned to his paper.

'Afternoon,' the man said, in Jim's direction but not exactly to him.

'Afternoon,' said Jim.

'Mind if I join you?'

Jim had no particular desire to talk, but was unable to summon the will to resist. 'If you like,' he said.

The man picked up his glass and paper and slid into a chair next to him.

'Gordon Towker,' he said.

'Jim Palmer.'

'Saw you here with the piece from Goody's the other day.'

Jim stiffened. 'Piece?' he said.

'You know, Liz Burridge. All right, isn't she?'

Jim was already regretting having spoken to him. He had a thin, sharp face, and a lipless mouth. He was losing his black hair, and what there was of it was plastered close to his skull. Jim looked at him for a moment without saying anything.

'Look here,' said Towker, 'I don't mean anything by it. She's just a bit of all right, that's all.'

'You could say that. I'm a married man, though.'

'Of course you are,' he said, with an expression Jim found hard to fathom.

They both took draughts of their beer.

'Working in Underhill's, then?' said Towker.

'That's right.'

'I've got a shop myself. On St Cuthbert Street.'

'What do you sell?'

'Oh, whatever comes along. Towker's Toys and Games, it's called. But I'll sell pretty much anything I think I can get rid of. Drop by some time and I'll show you around.'

'Thanks.'

They sat for a while looking at the other drinkers clustered by the bar.

'So what were you doing before you came here?' said Towker.

'I expect you know. Everyone else seems to.'

Towker smiled evasively. 'Yeah, I know. You had a Jaguar garage and it went bust.'

'So why ask?' said Jim.

'Just trying to be civil,' said Towker with a shrug.

'All right. I'm sorry.' Jim extended his hand and shook Towker's. 'Some people can be a bit funny about it, that's all.'

'Not me, mate. I know what it's like to be down on your luck.' Towker paused, and then added, 'I'm unlucky too.'

'You are?'

He tossed the *Sporting Life* onto a chair. 'Unlucky with the gee-gees, unlucky with the ladies. I even got sunk in the war.'

'You were in the navy?'

'Merchant marine. Atlantic convoys, and then the Murmansk Run. Froze my bollocks off.'

'Where were you sunk?'

'Off southern Ireland. We got picked up pretty quick by a destroyer, though. It wasn't so bad.'

'I was in Ireland during the war. Sat it out in an RAF signals camp in the north.'

'Everything was simple in those days,' said Towker. 'Not like now.'

'I suppose so,' said Jim. 'You wouldn't want to go back to them, though, would you?'

'Crikey, no.' Towker drained his glass. 'Well, nice to meet you. Maybe I'll see you in here another day. And if you've ever got anything you want to sell, just let me know.'

'I haven't got a single thing to sell,' said Jim. 'But thanks for the offer.'

★   ★   ★

On a grey, chilly morning, Margaret changed into the smartest skirt and jumper she still possessed and set off for Tanyard Cottage. She wanted to tell Leonora Vale what a success the kitten had been, that Sarah was now inseparable from it. She had christened it Lucy, even though none of them could tell what sex it was. It slept in a cardboard box by the stove, and was not permitted to leave the kitchen. Jim had seemed remarkably tolerant of it, but he drew the line at its sharing Sarah's bed.

Autumn was well along, and the leaves were turning. Margaret drew deeply on the cold, pure air. Mornings like this brought back memories of her days on the farm near Midsomer Norton during the war. That time seemed dream-like now. Everything had been potential: the war would end, they would win, a man would sweep her off her feet, and that would be that. And all those things happened; but that hadn't quite been that after all.

Miss Vale appeared not to recognize Margaret at first. Then she said, 'Come in, poppet,' and turned back into the house. The stench of the place seemed if anything stronger than it had been before. Miss Vale was wearing the same dirty blue smock she had worn on Margaret's first visit.

'Sarah loves her kitten,' she said as they sat down.

'Sarah?'

'My daughter. You gave her a kitten when we called last week.'

'Ah yes. Would she like some more?'

'Thank you, but I think perhaps one is enough.'

'One is never enough of anything. Surely

you must know that.'

Margaret looked around the stuffy room. Everything about it expressed the solitariness of this woman. There was no decoration or memento that said who she was.

'I'm not sure,' said Margaret.

'Oh yes. The Platonic ideal. The unity of the whole. Would you like a cup of tea?'

'Thank you.'

Margaret followed her into the kitchen. The fire in the stove was almost out, and it took an age for the kettle to boil.

'You said the other day that you'd been a ballet dancer,' said Margaret after a while.

'Not ballet, *dance*. Ballet is a false and preposterous art, hardly an art at all.' Miss Vale shuffled about the kitchen as she spoke, and her hand shook slightly as she poured tea into the cups. 'Whereas dance is the expression of truth and beauty through the instrument of the human body.'

'Yes, of course.'

'That's what Isadora taught us, and she was the greatest dancer the world has ever known.'

'You actually studied with Isadora Duncan?'

'I was one of her earliest pupils. She tried to set up a school in England, but she failed, and my parents sent me to Berlin to join her there.'

'How old were you?'

'Oh, about eight, as I recall.'

Her hand went continually to her hair. Now and then she would fix her glittering eyes on Margaret's and hold them for the longest time.

'That's very young, hardly older than Sarah.'

'Well, things were different then. And my parents were devoted to Isadora and her ideas.'

'What was she like?'

'She was like an angel. She wasn't really one of us. When she danced in those gauzy dresses she was just other-worldly.'

They returned to the sitting room and sat down again in the lumpy armchairs.

'And she taught you?'

'Well, she did when she was there. But she was usually travelling, especially after she met Paris Singer. We were taught mostly by her governesses.'

'Who was Paris Singer?'

'The sewing-machine heir. He gave her all the money for the schools. They had a child, but he drowned, poor thing, along with her daughter.' She wrapped the smock closely around her waist, hugging herself as she did so.

'I had no idea. She seems to have had a tragic life.'

'She was beyond tragedy,' said Miss Vale emphatically. 'Everything was sacrificed to her art.'

'How long did you stay with her school?'

'Oh, eight years or more. I was teaching the younger ones myself by the time I left. We lived in a beautiful villa near Beaulieu for most of the time. Then a couple of years after war broke out Isadora moved the school to America, and I decided to go to London.'

Margaret hesitated for a moment, and then said, 'I do hope you don't mind my asking you all these questions.'

'Not at all, poppet. I can tell you're an artist too.'

'I'm not an artist, I'm afraid. I wish I could say I were.'

'You may not think so, but I see it in you,' said Miss Vale.

'I can't imagine how. I mean . . . it's very kind of you to say so; but I'm simply a wife and a mother.'

'Isadora was a wife and a mother.'

'And a great dancer, as you said.'

Miss Vale gazed at Margaret intently for a few moments. 'So what happened?' she said.

'What happened?'

'How did a family like yours come to be living at Fosse's Farm?'

Margaret hesitated and then said, 'Oh, my husband had some troubles.'

'What sort of troubles?'

'He had a business that failed.'

'And is he a good husband?'

She felt both discomfited and somehow gratified by this directness. 'Of course he is,' she said.

'Men are often not at their best when they're in trouble.'

'No, perhaps not. But he's a good man.'

'I've no doubt he is.'

Margaret returned her stare. 'I ought to be going,' she said. 'There's a lot to do.'

'You must come back,' said Leonora Vale. 'I like you.'

* * *

'Let's go to the pub,' said Jim one Sunday morning. 'I feel cooped up in here.'

Neither Margaret nor Sarah wanted to join them, so Jim and Billy set out alone for the Fourways Inn. Billy chose a place in the garden from where they could see the tor shimmering in the morning light. They sat quietly for a while. Lately there had been an awkwardness between them that neither knew how to dispel.

'Tell me what you've been reading in those

books of yours,' said Jim at last.

'About Glastonbury?'

'Yes.'

Billy's face assumed an expression of great earnestness. He stroked his upper lip with his forefinger, composing himself.

'Well, there were Druids and people like that, when it was an island. Then there was Joseph. Not Jesus's father, another one. He was called Joseph of something. It's a hard word starting with A. Anyway, he brought the Holy Grail to Glastonbury.'

'What was the Holy Grail meant to be, exactly?'

'It was a cup. Jesus and the disciples had drunk from it. Then Joseph collected some of Jesus's blood in it, when he was on the cross. It was a special cup. He also had a stick, and when he stuck it in the ground it became a bush, with lots of flowers.'

'A hawthorn bush,' said Jim.

'You know that bit. It's still there, isn't it?'

'Well, a bush of some sort will be there.'

Billy waited for something more from his father, but it didn't come. 'Anyway,' he said eventually, 'Arthur's knights wanted to find the Holy Grail. They looked all over, and then Sir Galahad found it. But as soon as he found it he died and went to heaven.'

'What happened to the Holy Grail?'

'I think they lost it again. Only Sir Galahad really found it.'

Jim looked away into the distance. 'What do you think that means, that Galahad would die and go to heaven as soon as he found the Holy Grail?'

Billy screwed up his face and thought for a moment. 'It means he found it. He'd been looking for it for a long time. They all had. And then he found it.'

'So when you find what you're looking for, everything's over?'

'Yes, sort of.'

Jim turned away from him again. 'I'd say those stories about Joseph and Arthur and his lot are poppycock,' he said.

'No they're not.'

'They're myths, Billy. Do you know what a myth is? Something people make up so as to comfort themselves.'

'But what's wrong with that?'

Jim gazed down into his glass. 'What's wrong with it?' he said. 'It makes people content with what they've got.'

'Isn't that a good thing?'

'It depends. In the case of you and me, it's not a good thing at all.'

'Why?'

'Because we've got nothing, that's why.'

The expression on his father's face was hard now, and it frightened Billy.

'Let's go there and find out if those stories are true,' he said.

'We'd need a car.'

Billy glanced back at the tor. It seemed to be further away every time he looked at it.

'Why don't we have a car any more?' he said eventually.

'Because I don't sell them any more.'

'But lots of people who don't sell them have them, don't they?'

'Oh, I don't know what I'm saying.' Jim paused, and then tried again. 'We haven't got as much money as we used to.'

'Will we ever have one again?'

'I hope so.'

'I liked the smell of them. Especially the Jaguar.'

His father's features softened. 'I liked the smell of them too,' he said. 'All that walnut and leather.'

'If you sell a lot of clothes, perhaps we'll have enough money for one then.'

Jim sighed. 'I'd have to sell plenty of clothes to buy a Jaguar, Billy. A whole mountain of them.'

★ ★ ★

When Jim next dropped by the Star for a pint, Gordon Towker was sitting in the corner. He sat down beside him.

'Saintly Place,' said Towker.

'A saintly place?' said Jim. 'The Star?'

'No. In the three forty-five at Chepstow. Feel like a flutter?'

'I'm no good at betting,' said Jim. 'Never have been.'

'Well hang on while I phone through my bet. Then maybe you'd like to see the shop?'

Jim watched as Towker stalked out of the room and to the phone box. What a mug, he thought. Did anyone ever make any money betting on horses?

When Towker returned they walked to his shop. He unlocked the front door and swung the sign to 'open'. It was a sort of den, musty and with very little light, and cluttered from floor to ceiling. Jim noticed an old Dansette record player, a transistor radio, boxes of fireworks, and piles of *Picture Posts*, *Beanos* and *Dandys*. There were spare parts for bicycles, Subbuteo table-football games, Hornby train sets. And books, lots of them, some on shelves and others in stacks on the floor. Jim picked one up. *Young England*, it read on the cover, and inside, 'An Illustrated Annual for Boys

Throughout the English-Speaking World'.

The stack of books toppled, and Jim made to pick them up. 'Where do you get this stuff?' he said.

'Oh, all over. People around here know what I'm in the market for.'

'Do you ever sell any of it?'

Towker looked hurt. 'What do you mean, do I ever sell any of it?' he said. 'How do you think I live?'

'Sorry. It's just that . . . well, there's a lot here.'

'Ever occurred to you that there are six bloody schools in this town?'

'Yes, but I thought they were for well-off kids.'

'You'd be surprised. Tight bastards, some people, even if they do send their kids to fancy schools.'

Jim looked above his head. Model aeroplanes hung by strings from the ceiling.

'I'll do all right this week,' said Towker, 'selling Halloween stuff. Then it's Guy Fawkes Night. And then before you know it it'll be Christmas. There's always something going on.'

Towker began to pick up the books. What did he do in here all day? Jim wondered.

'I'd better be getting back,' he said. 'Thanks for showing me around.'

'I'll be seeing you in the Star, then,' said Towker.

* * *

Farmer Alton had confronted Frank Will-mott's father with the facts of his crime, and Frank had been given a thick ear. He had been surly with the other boys since. At break one morning Alan was telling them about the Biggles book he was reading. Billy could tell he was trying to mend things.

'It's called *Biggles Defies the Swastika*,' he said. 'It's fantastic. He gets trapped in Norway when the Jerries invade. He dresses up in a German uniform and pretends to be a Gestapo officer. Then he and Algy get caught by Biggles's enemy, Von somebody.'

'Do they get away?' said Les.

'Don't know yet, I haven't got that far.'

''Course they'll get away,' said Frank. 'It's Biggles, isn't it? He always wins in the end.'

'Anyway, it's smashing.'

Frank turned to Billy and said, 'What did your dad do in the war?'

'He was in the RAF,' said Billy.

'Oh yeah? My dad drove a tank. He was with Monty in North Africa. I bet he killed more Jerries than your dad did.'

'I don't know how many Jerries my dad

killed. But he was really brave.'

'I bet my dad was braver than yours.'

'No he wasn't.'

'Yes he was.'

'He wasn't, so there.'

'Prove it.'

'How?'

'In a fight. You and me. The winner's dad is the bravest.'

Billy looked at Frank. He was in for a fight, he knew it: the time had come. But Frank was bigger and stronger, and he was bound to lose.

'All right, then,' he said.

The other boys backed away, chanting 'fight, fight, fight', and then 'oih, oih, oih'. Frank raised his fists, and Billy did the same. Suddenly Frank leaped forward and lashed out, catching Billy painfully on the side of the face. Billy had never used fists before: whenever he'd had fights at the Unicorn they'd always been wrestling bouts.

Frank moved in again, this time punching Billy in the chest. Billy quickly realized he was beaten, but knew too that he must not give up just yet. He launched himself at Frank, pushing him to the ground, and fell on top of him. But Frank simply rolled them both over, straddling Billy and twisting his arm behind his back.

'Submit?' he said.

Billy was wincing with pain, but he said nothing. Frank pressed his arm even further up his back.

'Submit?'

'Submit.'

Frank climbed off him, triumph lighting up his face. Billy got up and dusted himself off.

'So, my dad's braver than yours,' said Frank. 'That proves it.'

Billy said nothing. He looked at Alan as if to appeal for his support, but it was clear that Alan was unable to give it.

'You have to say it,' said Frank, 'otherwise I'll clock you one again. My dad's braver than yours.'

'All right,' said Billy. 'Your dad's braver than mine.' He turned away from the other boys and tried to hold back his tears.

★   ★   ★

The day before the concert, Jim set off for work and then abruptly turned back. He walked through the kitchen, muttered, 'forgot something,' to Margaret, and went upstairs to the children's room. Taking Billy's Dinky toy sets from the cupboard, he hid them under his coat, and without another word left the house and set off for Wells.

During his lunch break, he went to the Star Hotel and looked in on the bar. Towker wasn't there, so he walked on to his shop. He was inside, leafing through an *Eagle* comic. Jim took out the Dinky toyboxes and laid them on the counter.

'My boy's,' he said. 'He's grown out of them. What'll you give me?'

Towker opened the boxes. One contained the five racing cars and the other five sports cars, including an MG, an Austin Healey and a Jaguar XK120. Towker examined them closely. They were indestructible, these cars, and didn't bear a single mark, despite the many accidents Billy had visited on them.

'Five bob,' said Towker.

'Each?'

'No, for both.'

'Come on, Towker, these things are valuable. They're gift sets, not just odd cars.'

'Seven.'

Jim looked down at the cars. He tried to remember what they had cost him three years ago or whenever it was he'd bought them. A lot more than seven shillings, certainly.

'Ten,' he said.

'Seven bob,' said Towker, turning his attention back to the *Eagle*. 'Take it or leave it.'

'Oh, all right then.'

Towker went into the back of the shop and returned with the money.

'Got anything else like these?'

Jim pocketed the coins. 'I'll talk to my boy and let you know,' he said.

★   ★   ★

He met Liz in the Crown for a drink before the concert. She had dolled herself up, with too much make-up and lacquer in her hair, and she was wearing a tight-fitting green dress. When she took off her coat Jim ran his eye down her lovely figure.

'Don't stare,' said Liz, smiling. 'It's rude.'

Jim shrugged. 'You look great, that's all,' he said. He watched her sip her cider. She was excited, he could tell. They walked to the Regal cinema. An oddly assorted crowd was gathering outside: middle-aged people, young couples, and even a lugubrious gang of Teddy boys. Jim brandished his tickets, and they made their way to their seats.

After a long wait the members of Eddie Calvert's band appeared and took up their places on the stage. There was a certain look to them all. They wore evening dress and slicked back their hair, and many of them had pencil moustaches. A chorus of four men and four women singers stepped out, flanking the musicians. Calvert himself bounded on stage, and immediately the band struck up the first number. A ripple of applause spread around the audience. Jim leaned over towards Liz and whispered, ' 'Zambesi'.'

They ran through their repertoire in a way that seemed pretty mechanical to Jim, the band members standing for their solos, the singers crooning, Calvert lifting his eyebrows in time with the phrases he played on his trumpet. In the cha-cha rhythms of 'Cherry Pink and Apple Blossom White', Jim thought they might fly off his face. The melodies flowed, and Jim's thoughts drifted towards the music he loved, towards Jimmy Dorsey's 'Tiger Rag' and Count Basie's 'One O'Clock Jump'. This was so tame by comparison. He looked across at Liz, and saw that she was rapt. Whatever else, it was good to have a pretty girl at his side.

The concert ended with Calvert's signature tune, 'Oh Mein Papa', a dirge that had somehow been a number-one hit. Everyone applauded loudly, and the band took several bows. As they made their way out of the cinema Jim was aware of the excited chatter around him. Evidently this sort of thing was sufficiently rare in Wells to cause a stir.

He took Liz to the Swan Hotel, calculating that he had just about enough to cover dinner provided they didn't drink too much. They were shown to their table by a spotty youth in an ill-fitting suit, and Jim ordered two glasses of white wine.

'I've never been to the Swan,' said Liz. 'Well, I've never been to a restaurant, not what you'd call a proper restaurant anyway.'

'It's the best place in town,' said Jim.

'I expect you've been to lots of places like this.'

'I suppose I have. But not for a while.'

There were very few other diners, and Jim was glad they would not be overheard: the illicit pleasures of the evening were tinged with feelings of guilt and anxiety he was unable to banish.

'So you enjoyed it,' he said.

'I loved it. I mean, it's not Tommy Steele, but it's just so good to hear music, isn't it, real music?'

'The radio and records don't give you that . . . oh, I don't know, that shivery feeling.'

'Have you heard a lot of bands?'

'Not really. Bath was never much of a place for the kind of music I like. The best concert I ever went to was in London.'

'Who did you see?'

'Louis Armstrong, at the Palladium. Now that was a *concert*.'

Their food came. Jim was famished, and

began eating straight away. He continued to do most of the talking throughout dinner. He was enjoying himself, enjoying impressing this girl with his stories. She made him feel he'd led an interesting life, that the state of affairs he now found himself in was merely temporary, and would one day add to his fund of anecdotes.

After dinner he walked Liz to her parents' house. All the lights were out. 'I don't suppose I can come in?' he said.

'No, I don't think that would be a good idea.' She hesitated for a moment, and then said, 'Next week they're away.'

Jim looked at her intently, and kissed her wide mouth. She held back for a moment, and then folded herself into him. He kissed her again, prolonging it until she broke off. 'Good night,' she said, and turned towards the door.

'Until next week, then,' said Jim.

3

In the school yard there was a tacit understanding that since the fight some sort of order had been restored. But Billy was burning with resentment, certain that he was better than Frank, just not sure how to show it.

'Alan,' he said quietly as they leaned against the wall of the playground. 'Could we get to Glastonbury Tor, just you and me?'

'You mean walk?'

'No, it's too far. Could we hitch a ride?'

Alan's eyes gleamed. 'Sure. We could walk to the main road and stick out our thumbs. Somebody's bound to pick us up, I reckon.'

'We'll have to pretend to our parents that we're going somewhere else.'

'Easy. We're collecting pennies for the guy.'

Alan called for him at the weekend. Billy was sure this was the bravest thing he'd ever done. On the main road between Pilton and Glastonbury there were very few cars in either direction, and none of them stopped. After half an hour they sat down at the side of the road and began to throw stones into a stream, turning back every time they heard the sound of a car.

'We're too little,' said Alan. 'They don't think we mean it.'

'What if we stand in the middle of the road?'

'No fear.'

They stared into the water.

'Why's it so important to go to the tor?' said Alan.

'I don't know . . . it's like Kirrin Island is for the Famous Five. It's a special place.'

'But *why* is it a special place?'

Billy looked towards the tor. It was encircled by mist today, and seemed to float in the air.

'What about all the stories?' he said. 'Why have so many things happened there? It must be the most special place in England.'

A pale blue Morris Minor appeared, and it slowed and came to a halt. For a moment Billy's spirits soared. The door opened and a woman stepped out.

'Crumbs,' said Alan. 'It's Mrs Hardie, the vicar's wife.'

'Alan Tyler?' said the woman. 'What on earth are you doing?'

'Just going for a walk,' said Alan.

'Then why were you trying to flag down a car?'

'We were tired,' said Billy.

Mrs Hardie frowned at them. 'Then you would do better to try getting a ride in the right direction. Come on, I'll take you home.'

From the moment Mrs Hardie's car pulled up outside the cottage it became impossible to maintain the deception of collecting pennies for the guy. His father sent Billy to his room, where he waited for ages before he heard footsteps on the stairs. Worse than any punishment was this time of dread, this time of rehearsing excuses and wondering what his father would say to him.

'Let's get two things straight,' said Jim, his face flushed with anger. 'Firstly, you don't lie to your mother and me about where you're going, and you never try to cadge lifts. God knows who might have picked you up: there are some very strange people around these days. And secondly, you must get out of your head this stupid idea of going to the tor. It's only a bloody hill, after all.'

Billy usually knew better than to answer back; but today he felt stubborn, and refused to be cowed.

'It's not just a hill,' he said. 'And those stories aren't poppycock, like you said.'

'Listen, young man. If I hear any more nonsense about the tor, it's going to be out of bounds for ever.'

Billy lay in bed that night unable to sleep,

images of Glastonbury teeming in his mind. I will go there, he said to himself, I will go there.

★ ★ ★

Margaret stopped by Leonora Vale's cottage on the way to the village shop and gave her some fresh milk for the cats.

'How sweet of you.'

'What do you feed them, usually?'

'Oh, scraps, mostly. They take care of themselves. They are hunters, after all. You should see what some of them bring in. One dragged a vole back once.'

They went through the ritual of making tea. When they had sat down Miss Vale said, 'Well, how are you?'

Margaret was unable to suppress a sigh. 'I'm all right, I suppose,' she said. She looked across at Miss Vale, who was studying her closely. 'Well no, I'm not all right.' The ghost of a smile hovered around her mouth.

'Do you know the radio programme called *Mrs Dale's Diary*?'

'I listen to it every day.'

'You know how she's always saying, 'I'm worried about Jim'?'

'And she has plenty to worry about.'

Margaret absently brushed cat hairs from

her skirt. 'Well, I'm worried about Jim,' she said.

'Of course you are. Jim's worried about Jim.'

Margaret was startled. 'You know?'

'I don't know anything, except what I see in you. I've never set eyes on your husband. But he's lost, isn't he?'

With these words Margaret simply crumpled. It was as though all the anxiety and sadness of the past months were being released at once. Leonora Vale sat down beside her on the threadbare settee and put her arm around her shoulders. 'Now, poppet, you're going to tell me all about it,' she said. 'But first I think you need a little something.'

She went into the kitchen and returned with a hip flask, pouring dark brown liquid into the milky tea. 'Have a slug of that,' she said, and then she poured even more into her own cup. Margaret drank the bitter stuff and wiped her eyes. They sat in silence for a while, Leonora Vale watching Margaret thoughtfully.

'He's never had a strong sense of who he is, that's the problem. He sees himself as the world reflects him back.'

'Most people do.'

'But with Jim it's worse. Anyway, when things were going his way he was fine. Oh, he was arrogant sometimes; but he was settled in himself. Since the bankruptcy he seems . . . well, as you say, he's lost.'

'He needs your help.'

'But how do I give it to him? He's becoming a stranger to me. We don't . . . ' Margaret looked up at her and knew that nothing less than the truth would do. 'We don't make love any more. We barely talk to each other.'

'Forgive me, but this is a very common experience. All men and women go through something like this at some time in their lives.'

'It's happened to you?'

Leonora Vale smiled wryly. 'It's happened to me,' she said. 'A few times.'

'You were married?'

'Just once. Marriage didn't seem the be all and end all in the world I lived in. But one man did persuade me to throw my lot in with him.'

'Who was he?'

'His name was Lawrence James. He was a choreographer.' She smiled again. 'He literally swept me off my feet.'

'How long were you married?'

'Four years. But we were often not even in the same place. And for him it was an open marriage.'

'Open?'

'He could sleep with whomever he pleased, and I wasn't to mind.'

'And did you mind?'

'I minded terribly. We were supposed to have yielded to an over-powering love for each other, a love that would be equal to anything. We were Tristan and Iseult. But it wasn't long before I knew he was making love to someone else.'

'How did you know?'

Leonora Vale gave her an enigmatic look. 'You just know, don't you?'

Margaret returned her gaze for a moment. 'I've usually known,' she said, 'when Jim has been seeing someone else.'

'Of course you have. They can't hide it.'

Margaret was getting a taste for her whisky-laced tea. She held the mug in both hands and rocked slowly back and forth. How strangely comforting was this eccentric woman.

When it was time to go, Leonora Vale walked with her to the gate. She took Margaret's head in her hands and gently kissed her forehead. 'You must talk to him,' she said.

★   ★   ★

It was becoming something of a habit now for Jim to go to the Star for a pint at lunchtime. At first he had promised himself this would be an occasional treat, but his need to get away from Reg and the shop, and for some sort of company, drove him there almost every day. Towker was always lounging around. Jim had become a little wary of him since he'd sold the Dinky toys, and sometimes he deliberately sat as far away from him as he could. He did so today, but soon Towker collected his pint and came over to join him.

'Afternoon,' he said.

'Hello,' said Jim.

Towker methodically rolled a cigarette. 'Everything all right?' he said eventually.

'As well as can be expected.'

'Hear you were at the Eddie Calvert concert.'

Jim sensed trouble looming. 'Yes, I was.'

'Good, was it?' He picked some shreds of tobacco from his lower lip.

'It was good for what it was. He's not exactly my sort of thing.'

'She enjoyed it, did she?'

Jim thought for a moment how best to handle this. Dismissively, he decided. 'Yes, she did. Calvert's a bit old-fashioned for her, though.'

'They just like being taken out though, don't they, women? Like being shown a good time.'

Towker took a silver lighter from his pocket and made several attempts to light his meagre cigarette. Jim tried to keep his temper. He knew he was fooling himself if he thought his seeing Liz might go unnoticed.

'Expensive, though,' said Towker when Jim didn't reply.

'Expensive?'

Towker finally lit the cigarette, and drew on it deeply. 'Women,' he said. 'Cost the bloody earth.'

'I suppose they do.'

Jim was about to drain his glass and stand up when Towker spoke again.

'I don't suppose you've got anything else to sell me like those Dinkys?'

'No, I haven't. I'll ask the boy some time, but nothing at the moment.'

Towker glanced across the room. Something held Jim back, he couldn't say what.

'But you could use some cash, I expect.'

'We all could.'

'Yeah, but you especially, if you don't mind my saying so. What's Underhill paying you?'

'I don't think that's any of your business.'

'Sorry. But you know what I mean — kids, and then a night out now and then.'

'Yes, I know what you mean.' Once again Jim made to leave, but stayed fast in his chair.

'You wouldn't want to do a freelance job, would you, on the side?'

Towker was by now looking thoroughly shifty. Jim felt a wave of revulsion pass over him. 'What sort of job?' he heard himself saying.

'Driving. Delivering something.'

'Why can't you do it yourself?'

'I don't have a car. Can't drive, anyway.'

'Well I don't have a car either, in case you hadn't noticed.'

'But you could get one, couldn't you? You could borrow one?'

Jim sat back wearily. 'What are you talking about?' he said.

'I've just got something needs delivering to London, that's all. Something I can't sell in the shop.'

'What is it?'

'Now that would be telling.'

'Yes it bloody well would. If you think I'm going to run an errand for you without even knowing what it is, you can think again.'

Towker sucked on his cigarette. 'Twenty quid,' he said.

'Twenty quid?'

'For a day's outing to London.'

Jim looked down at his hands. Twenty

pounds was almost three weeks' wages.

'What if I said yes?' said Jim. 'What if I got hold of a car?'

Towker exhaled sharply. 'You come round to the lock-up,' he said, 'load some packages, drive them to an address I'll give you in Bloomsbury, and I give you twenty quid in cash.'

Jim looked angrily at Towker. 'Fuck off,' he said, and he stood up and strode out into the street.

★   ★   ★

Billy crept down the stairs and out into the yard. It was dark in the mornings now, an enveloping dark he hadn't known when they lived on the edge of a city. Hubert Fosse had set up hurricane lamps in the milking shed, which hissed and spat now and then. He had been washing down the cows, and they steamed in the dim light.

Billy stood in the doorway watching his mother rhythmically milking a cow. It was restless, and stamped its hind hooves. Margaret spoke to it soothingly but was unable to calm it. Eventually she turned and saw him staring at her through the gloom.

'Billy?' she said.
'Hello, Mum.'

'Why are you down so early?'

'I couldn't sleep.'

She twisted herself around to look at him.

'Are you all right?'

Billy stood for a few moments without speaking. There were things he had wanted to tell someone for quite a while, but now that the moment had come he felt tongue-tied. Finally he said, 'Mum, what do you do when someone doesn't like you very much?'

Margaret stopped milking and turned on the stool to face him. 'Come here,' she said. Billy stepped towards her, and she held out her hands to him.

'Who doesn't like you?'

'There's a boy . . . ' Billy took a deep breath. 'There's a boy called Frank Willmott at school. We had a fight. He said his dad was braver than mine.'

'Well that's exactly the sort of silly thing that boys say, isn't it? It doesn't mean anything.'

'But he really doesn't like me, Mum.'

She stroked Billy's hands in hers.

'Then *you* must be brave,' she said. 'Why do you think he doesn't like you?'

'I don't know. Because I read books. And because he thinks I'm a liar.'

'A liar?'

'Yes, when I talk about what we used to do

before we came here.'

'I expect our old life must seem strange to someone like Frank Willmott,' said Margaret. 'You must think carefully about what you say. You haven't been boasting, have you?'

'No, Mum. But I did talk about the Jaguars.'

'Well there you are, then.' She raised a hand to his hair and brushed it back. 'Things are very different now, Billy. It's best to try to forget how they were before. You do like it here in the country, don't you?'

'Yes, I do. It's just that . . . ' He looked at her questioningly. 'Mum, why did we come here? Why didn't we just stay where we were?'

His mother sighed. 'Your father explained that to you, Billy. He had to close the garage and find another job, and this is where he found one.'

'But *why* did he have to close the garage?'

'Well, because . . . ' Margaret hesitated. 'Because he made some mistakes.'

Billy looked around the shed, at the cows that flanked them on all sides. 'I don't think Frank believes we ever had a garage,' he said.

'It doesn't matter. You'd be better off simply not talking about it. Try to talk to him about the things *he's* interested in.'

'I don't think he's interested in anything, except pushing other boys around.'

'Every school has its Frank, doesn't it? The Unicorn must have had a Frank.'

'I don't remember. There wasn't anyone who hated me there.'

She rested her hands on his shoulders. 'He doesn't hate you, Billy, no one hates you. He's just a boy. You have to show him that you're brave, and then he'll like you.'

'How do I show him I'm brave?'

'By being yourself. And by not getting into fights.'

'I didn't want to fight.'

'Then you should have turned your back.'

Billy looked down at the ground. 'I'll try,' he said. 'I'll try to be brave.'

'Good.' His mother hugged him, and stood up. 'Now, I have two more cows to milk. Why don't you go and lay the table for breakfast?'

Billy ran out into the yard. The faint light of dawn led him back to the cottage, where his father and sister were still asleep. The image of his mother patiently drawing milk from the cow's udder stayed vividly in his mind.

★ ★ ★

In the crowded bar of the Crown, Jim sat with Liz in a glazed silence. The knowledge that her parents' house stood empty not far away was strangely daunting to him. There didn't seem to be much to talk about, and they found themselves taking an excessive interest in the old photographs and prints on the walls. The publican glanced over at them now and then, smiling crookedly. We attract attention, Jim thought, there's no getting away from it. Did he seem *that* much older than her? Chewing his sausages and baked beans, he found himself thinking back to his conversation with Gordon Towker, to the things he'd said about women and money. They stepped out into the chilly night, and Jim took Liz by the hand as they walked to her home.

She ushered him into the sitting room, looking up at him shyly as he entered. There was a brown three-piece suite with white antimacassars, a green-tiled fireplace, an ornate dark-wood clock on the mantelpiece, and a small Ekco television set. China cats and dogs sat on the surfaces of tables and shelves, along with photographs, mostly of Liz as a girl. She was an adored only child, it was easy to see.

'Tea?' she said.

'Have you got anything stronger?'

Liz went into the kitchen and reappeared with a bottle of Cyprus sherry.

'Tea, then,' said Jim.

When she returned she perched herself on the other end of the settee. Jim was tense, and unsure of himself. In the old days he would have been master of a situation like this. Eventually he laid down his cup and slid along the settee towards her, putting an arm around her shoulders and kissing her tentatively. She responded readily, raising a hand to his face and pressing her mouth to his. 'Let's go upstairs,' he said. He hated the grapplings of the settee, the awkward baring of a breast or raising of a skirt, the breaking off in a fluster so as to get to the bed. A man should undress a woman slowly and tenderly.

Liz led him up to her room. The bed was very narrow.

'What about your parents' room?'

'Oh no, I couldn't.'

She switched on the bedside lamp and turned to face him. They embraced and kissed again, and Jim began to take off her blouse and skirt. The outlines of her body were soft in the shadows, her skin creamy and warm. Jim suddenly felt a hunger he hadn't known in a long time. She lay on the bed, and he hurriedly undressed. When they were naked he forgot everything he had said to himself downstairs, everything he had ever known about this act except its culmination. His urgency made him clumsy, and Liz even had to remind him to put on a rubber. It was over very quickly.

They lay for a while, Jim resting his head on her shoulder, unable to look her in the eye. This was what you did with a tart, he thought, this taking and using. But Liz was a sweet, trusting and inexperienced girl.

'It's all right,' she said, running her hand through his hair.

'No it's not, Liz. That might as well have been my first time.'

'Don't be silly.' She kissed him lightly.

Jim raised himself on his elbow and gazed down at her.

'Except my first time, I couldn't even get it up.'

She laughed, and kissed him again. 'Next time will be different,' she said.

He left soon after, and walked back to Underhill's to collect his bicycle. As he cycled out of town he rehearsed the conversation he would have with Margaret when he got home, the lies about another night out with the lads from the Star. He imagined her curled up by the fireplace with her book. And he wondered what she might be thinking, about him, about the children, about everything.

★ ★ ★

On Guy Fawkes Night they set off for the village. Billy insisted on holding the torch, even though there was a full moon and it really wasn't necessary. He shone it into the hedges and trees, and up into the sky. 'It's like an umbrella of light,' he said.

There was a crowd of people milling around under the apple trees, and at the top of the huge bonfire a gaunt-looking guy sat strapped to a chair. A group of children were chanting, 'Guy, guy, guy, Stick him up on high; Hang him on a lamp post, And leave him there to die.'

They saw the Misses Shute, and walked over to them.

'Well, Billy and Sarah,' said the thin Miss Shute. 'And Mr and Mrs Palmer. How nice to see you all.'

Seeing his teachers in this dramatic setting changed Billy's idea of them. They wore their long black dresses, as they always did, but there was something different about them here, an ease and a familiarity that was quite absent at school. Alan had told him they had been in the village for thirty years, an unimaginably long time.

'Do you think Miss Shute will ride on her broom tonight?' whispered Sarah to Billy.

'No, that's at Halloween. Anyway, she hasn't got a broom.'

'We didn't do anything at Halloween, did we? We used to have a pumpkin.'

'I don't think they have pumpkins around here.'

Billy and Sarah stayed close to their parents. Many of their friends were there, including Alan Tyler, but they all remained with their own families. Frank and Ed Willmott looked subdued as they stood by their father, who towered over them. He's the giant in *Jack in the Beanstalk*, thought Billy. He looked up at Jim, who though quite tall himself was overshadowed by Willmott. He hoped they wouldn't get into a fight.

A man took a long pole with a stuffed sock on the end, dipped it in a can of oil, and set a match to it. It leaped into flame, and he thrust it into the bonfire. It had been dry lately, and the wood kindled easily. Within less than a minute it was roaring, the guy and the chair consumed by the flames, and sparks flew into a sky turned suddenly bright orange. After the fire's first rush, people stepped forward with potatoes on sticks and laid them in the ashes. Then the fireworks began, rockets and cascades and roman candles.

'Can I light a firework?' said Sarah.

'No,' said Jim. 'But you can have a sparkler. I'll get you one.'

She ran in circles waving the sparkler, stopping now and then to watch rockets whoosh into the sky. Jim helped light and launch them: Mighty Atoms, Rockets, Silver Rains. He took a match to one that stood in a milk bottle, and it shot up and exploded into hundreds of points of light. Billy and Sarah gasped, and begged him to light another.

He straightened the rocket, lit the fuse and stood back. Just at that moment, the bottle gently tipped over onto its side. Jim lunged forwards in an attempt to right it, but he was too late, and it caught light and hurtled towards Sarah, grazing the side of her face as it went. She let out a cry of pain, and he dashed towards her, taking her head in his hands. There was a burn mark that seared her cheek and ear, and her hair was scorched. He picked her up and held her close to him. Her body was convulsed with crying.

'She's in shock,' he said to Margaret. 'We must get her to a doctor straight away.'

Margaret ran over to the Shute sisters. In the noise and confusion no one else was aware of what had happened.

'Dr Enright,' said the thin Miss Shute. 'His house is less than a mile away. Follow me.'

They hurried out into the road. Jim held Sarah tight and whispered to her soothingly, while Margaret grasped Billy's hand. By now

Sarah was sobbing quietly, burying her face in Jim's chest. Billy looked on, wondering how brave he might have been had the rocket hit him rather than his sister.

Dr Enright was a soft-faced man in his sixties. He took one look at Sarah and led her into the surgery room that was attached to his house. He said almost nothing, tutting now and then to himself. Sarah squinted in the bright light while Enright took out some astringent and a cotton swab. 'This will sting, child,' he said, and Sarah recoiled and cried out again when he rubbed her cheek. Billy stood by, watching attentively.

'An inch to the right and she might have lost an eye,' said Enright. 'As it is, this will heal quickly. You are most fortunate.' He said this to Jim rather than to Sarah.

Jim let out a long, slow breath, and sat down on a chair. 'Thank God,' he said, holding his head in his hands.

'It wasn't your fault,' said Margaret. 'It could have happened to anyone.'

'Of course it was my fault, Maggie,' he said angrily. 'It was bloody stupid of me not to make sure the bottle was stable.'

'It's a dangerous night, Fireworks Night,' said Enright. 'I always expect a visitor or two. It's easy to be careless.'

Sarah was whimpering gently. Margaret

took her up in her arms. 'It's all right now,' she said. 'Let's take you home.'

Enright ran them back to the cottage in his Alvis, Sarah sitting on Margaret's lap, Billy beside them.

'That's the last time I'm lighting any fireworks,' said his father.

* * *

Jim and Billy set out early the following Saturday and cycled to Wells, Billy balancing precariously on the crossbar. They arrived at Reg's house before eight, and he gave Jim the keys to the Vanguard.

'I don't want you giving it any poke, now,' he said.

'I'll take it easy,' said Jim, 'I promise.'

Reg watched as Jim and Billy opened the doors and slid into the front seats.

'Do you really think you're going to get anything out of your Aunt Beatrice?' he said.

'I just want to make up, that's all.'

Reg eyed him thoughtfully. 'Well, good luck,' he said. As Jim engaged first gear and gingerly steered the car out into the road, he shouted, 'And no poke, now, do you hear?'

They drove through the half-light and came to a halt outside a lockup garage. Billy saw a dim figure emerge from the scrubby wasteland on the other side of the road.

'Morning,' the man said. He surveyed the car. 'That'll do. Nice big boot.' Then he saw Billy sitting in the passenger seat, and looked quizzically at Jim.

'Don't worry about the boy,' said his father. 'He wants to see his great-aunt.'

Billy looked at the man and decided he didn't like him one little bit. And it wasn't true that he wanted to see Aunt Beatrice: his father had insisted that he come.

The man opened the doors of the lock-up and brought out six packages wrapped in paper and tied up with string. They were heavy, and by the time they were loaded into the boot of the car it sat noticeably closer to the ground, the rear tyres subsiding a little into the tarmac. He gave Jim a scrap of paper.

'He'll be expecting you around lunchtime,' he said. 'He doesn't know your name, and he won't ask. All right?'

Jim looked up at him and nodded. 'Don't expect us back before seven or eight,' he said.

Sitting in the front seat of a car was a pleasure that Billy had imagined he would never know again. He watched the semaphore movements of his father's arms as he shifted the gears and swung the steering wheel. Wanting to play his part in this show of dexterity, he reached out to the dials of the radio and gave them a reverent touch.

'Don't fiddle,' said Jim sharply.

Billy looked across at him, and instantly the joy he had been feeling drained away. His father was hunched over the wheel, an anxious expression on his face. He was so unlike the relaxed and confident driver Billy had always known.

'About those packages,' he said. 'We're not delivering them, understand?'

'What do you mean?'

'I mean that as far as your mother and sister and great-aunt are concerned, we didn't pick up any packages and we're not dropping off any packages. Do I have to make it any plainer than that?'

'But we are.'

'Yes, Billy, you and I know that we are. But nobody else is to know. And if you tell anyone, you're for it. That man's a friend of mine, and I'm doing him a favour. But he doesn't want it talked about, and that's that.'

By now they were passing through the Georgian terraces of Bath. This was where they had once lived, in a big house with a Jaguar parked in the drive; this was where they had been happy. He folded his arms and fell silent.

London had always been something of a mystery to Jim, and it took a long time to find the place in Bloomsbury where they were going. He parked in Museum Street and they strolled to a bookshop. 'Bernard Smith, Antiquarian & Second-hand Bookseller' read the sign, and on the door a note said, 'Back in ten minutes'. Billy peered through the window, surveying the books on display. Macaulay's History of England stood in four uniform volumes, The Memoirs of Giacomo Casanova in twelve. There were sets of Shakespeare and George Bernard Shaw. He looked up and down the street: every second shop sold books or prints. There must be thousands of books here, he thought, tens of thousands.

A middle-aged man appeared, and looked at them warily. He was plump and dishevelled, his green corduroy jacket worn at the elbows, the lapels sprinkled with cigarette ash. He took a keyring from his pocket and opened the door. They followed him inside without a word passing between them.

'I'm delivering something,' said Jim as the bookseller turned on the lights. The spaces between the stacks of books were narrow, the shelves extending to the high ceiling.

'You would be the man from Somerset,' said Smith.

'I would be the man from the man from Somerset,' said Jim.

Smith opened up the till and inspected its contents. He laid a brown paper bag on the counter and took out a sandwich, biting into it hungrily.

'Well, you'd better bring them in,' he said.

Jim stepped back into the street and returned with two of the packages. By the time he had brought back the other four, Smith was inspecting the contents of the first package closely. He turned the pages of a book carefully, nodding his head in a bird-like way as he viewed them through the half-glasses on the end of his nose. Billy sensed this process was going to take a while, and he sat down on a stool. Smith leafed through the books one by one, now and then taking another bite of the sandwich and wiping his fingers carefully on a handkerchief before resuming. Billy wasn't able to see many of the titles, but he could read the names Defoe, Richardson, Smollett.

The silence was interrupted only by an occasional rasping sound as Smith cleared his throat. Eventually he looked up at Jim. 'Very fine,' he said, 'very fine indeed.' He disappeared for a moment and returned with an envelope. 'There's no need to open it. Your man and I have an understanding.'

Billy watched as Jim slipped the envelope into his jacket pocket. There was only one thing it could contain, surely, and that was money.

'Good day,' said Smith, and he began to carry the books into the back of the shop.

'Good day,' said Jim, grasping the handle of the door. Then he looked back. 'Is this a good business, books?'

Smith glanced up at him, taking the glasses from his nose.

'It is if you know what you're doing,' he said.

'I suppose that's true of any business.'

'I suppose it is.'

Jim gazed thoughtfully for a moment at the rows of books, and then nodded to Billy to step out into the street. As the door shut behind them, Billy wondered what on earth his father was up to.

⋆　⋆　⋆

Beatrice Palmer, Billy's maiden great-aunt, lived in a Victorian mansion block on the bank of the Thames. They parked near Putney Bridge and walked to the entrance, climbing two flights of stairs to the flat.

'Good afternoon, Jim,' said Beatrice, and to Billy, 'and you too, young man. How nice.'

'Hello, Aunt Bea.'

'Sit down and I'll make some tea.'

Beatrice was seventy now, and as elegant as always, in a blue and white polka-dot dress and black shoes. Jim followed her into the kitchen, and Billy went over to the balcony window. It was one of those brilliant afternoons when winter still seems benign, and a silvery light glinted on the surface of the river. They used to come here every year to watch the Boat Race, Beatrice preparing a high tea that was practically a banquet, with sandwiches, jellies, cakes and scones. Today, however, she handed Jim a cup and Billy a glass of lemonade without ceremony. Jim sank into a plush red velvet armchair, and then struggled to sit up straight.

'I received your letter,' she said. 'What did you want to say to me?'

Jim looked over at Billy and said, 'Why don't you go out onto the balcony and watch the boats?'

It was mild enough to sit outside on the wicker chairs. Billy placed his lemonade on the table and gazed out at the pleasure boats gliding by. He looked back through the glass door at his father and great-aunt, and jammed it open a little with his foot so as to hear their conversation.

'I wanted to say I'm sorry, more or less,' said Jim.

Beatrice examined him critically. 'I think

the moment for that has passed, don't you?' she said.

'I tried to apologize at the time.'

'Not very hard, as I recall.' She sipped her tea delicately.

'It was difficult.'

'It was indeed.'

'Aunt Bea, I know I didn't behave very well. But it wasn't all my fault.'

'Then whose fault was it, exactly?'

He seemed to cast about him for inspiration. 'It was the times. The credit squeeze. The rationing.'

'Jim, you made one miscalculation after another,' she said. 'Once you saw trouble looming you could quite easily have averted it. In the end the bank had no alternative but to call in your debts.'

His hands were gripping his knees tightly, and his expression was agitated. 'I'm sorry about your money, Aunt Bea,' he said. 'I would gladly repay it if I could.'

'You'll never be in a position to repay it, not in my lifetime.'

Jim glanced in Billy's direction, and Billy looked away.

'How is Margaret?' said Beatrice.

'Oh, fine. She seems to be coping.'

'I trust you understand how hard this must have been for her?'

'Of course I do.'

'I wonder about that.'

She stood up and crossed to the balcony door.

'Come back in, Billy,' she said. 'You'll catch cold.'

'I'm all right,' he said, not wanting to be drawn into this unsettling encounter.

'Tell me about your new school.'

Billy reluctantly stepped back into the room. 'It's very small,' he said. 'And I don't have to wear a uniform.'

'Do you like it?'

Billy shrugged, and looked at his father.

'You'd rather be back at the Unicorn, wouldn't you?'

'I suppose so,' said Billy. He had an impulse to talk about Frank Willmott, but then decided against it.

'But you miss your old life, I expect,' said Beatrice.

'Some things I miss.' He looked very directly at his great-aunt. 'I wish we had a car,' he said. 'Then we could all visit you like we used to. Today we're only borrowing Uncle Reg's Standard, and it's not much of a car anyway.'

'Billy, we've been through this a hundred times,' said Jim, setting down his teacup in a gesture of exasperation.

'Nevertheless the boy misses it,' said Beatrice. She patted her mouth with a napkin, and stood up to close the balcony door. Turning to face them again she said, 'I don't think I want you to come here again, Jim. If Margaret would like to bring the children she is welcome to.'

Billy looked at his father, who sat speechless in his chair.

'I'm sorry to have to say this in front of you, Billy,' she continued, 'but you must understand that there are some things in life that have consequences.'

Jim slowly got to his feet and motioned to Billy to follow him. Before he could make a move, Beatrice stepped across the room and kissed him on the cheek. He looked up at her, bewildered.

'I think you ought to be on your way home,' she said. 'It gets dark so early these days.'

They descended the stairs, and returned to the riverbank. Jim leaned against the wall, gazing vacantly into the water. A lighter was making its way upstream, pushing against the current. Billy looked up at Jim as though at a stranger. This day had made him feel afraid of his father. He watched the traffic crossing the bridge, and willed him to return to Reg's car. The trip was ruined now.

Whenever Billy had things on his mind he went for a walk. And he had things on his mind now, things that were difficult to understand. He clambered over the stile across the road and took in the familiar view. Seeing the countryside unfold below made him feel that it was there for him alone. The light was forever changing things, making the scene different every time he looked at it. Mostly it was like a great green carpet, but sometimes it was like old brown linoleum, and at others even a gold cloth. Always the tor loomed in the distance, a kind of sentinel.

From the first field he could see Coombe Hall, which was hidden from the road by a high wall and gates. It was a very large place, with a sweeping gravel drive, neatly tended lawns and gardens, and what looked like a dovecote at the back. Billy wondered who lived there, and why his father and mother had never spoken about them. In Bath he was always being taken to other people's houses, some quite as grand as this, where he dutifully played with children he didn't know or like while his parents sat talking for hours on end. Apart from Hubert Fosse and Miss Vale he knew no one here outside school. His mother seemed to want to get to know people, but his father showed no interest whatsoever.

What *was* his father interested in? he thought. And what was that strange day in London all about? He'd been told that Aunt Beatrice was particularly looking forward to seeing him; but when they arrived it seemed that she hadn't been expecting him at all. His father had wanted something from her, he was sure, something she was unwilling to give. And then there were the books, the secret books. Billy generally liked secrets; but this was not one he wanted to be in on.

He came to the ford by the school, and looked at the piece of rope that hung from a tree above it. He had often wondered whether he might be able to swing across to the other side, and now, seeing as there was no one watching him, he decided to give it a try. He stepped into the water, wading out to the middle. It was icy cold, and came up to his knees. He grabbed the rope and drew it back towards the bank. The bough of the tree creaked as he skimmed over the surface, but the rope didn't take him anywhere near the other side, and he found himself dangling in mid-air. He fell back into the stream and stumbled to the bank, where he stood trying to wring the water from his shorts.

He decided to walk up the Arminster road,

and soon he came upon a very large farm, with outbuildings that extended in every direction. It was like a fort, but an abandoned one, after the Indians had laid siege to it and killed all the whites. As he was imagining the terrible scenes of the massacre he heard familiar voices, and he turned to see Frank and Les striding down the hill, looking purposeful. When they saw Billy they glanced at one another and smiled conspiratorially.

'Billy Palmer,' said Frank.

'Hello.' They were the last people Billy wanted to see, and he made to walk past them. But Frank and Les stepped across the road and barred his way.

'Where are you off to, then?' said Frank.

'Just exploring.'

'Well this is our patch, so you can explore somewhere else.' Frank folded his arms and stared at Billy, and Les did the same. Billy thought for a moment what to do. There was no point in trying to pass, but at the same time he didn't want to turn around meekly and walk back down, no doubt being closely followed. He saw a path a few yards away that appeared to lead towards the village.

'I'm going to the shop, anyway,' he said, 'to get some things for Mum.'

'Shop's not open on Sundays,' said Frank, and he and Les sniggered.

Billy cursed himself for making such a stupid mistake. 'Oh, I forgot,' he said.

'So you'd better turn back then, hadn't you, and run along home.' Frank looked down at the dark stains on Billy's shorts. 'Been wetting yourself?' he asked, and he and Les began sniggering again.

'I was trying to swing across the river by the school.'

'Me Tarzan, you Jane,' said Les. By now he and Frank were laughing out loud. Billy felt mortified, and stood gazing at the ground.

A van appeared, and honked loudly. Frank and Les stepped to one side of the road, and Billy to the other. As the van passed, Billy saw his chance, and began to run alongside it up the hill. He had run twenty yards or so before the others realized what he'd done. They shouted at him, and gave chase. Billy was a good runner, and he was spurred on both by fear and by a determination to show them what he was capable of. He ducked into a side road, which began to take him downhill again. His heart was bursting, but he kept on. Looking back, he saw that he was leaving Frank and Les behind. The rush of cold air on his face thrilled him, and he ran even faster.

When a bend in the road took him out of their sight, he vaulted a gate and ran back across an empty field, hiding behind a tree at the bottom. He heard Frank and Les carrying on along the road, shouting his name and threatening to get him. Billy stood gasping, his hand resting on the rough bark. He saw that the field below would bring him out onto the Coombe road, and he ran towards the stone wall. Jumping over it, he was suddenly back on home ground, on the road he took every day to school. He made himself slow down, tried to saunter along this familiar road. But he wasn't very good at sauntering, and as soon as he had got his breath back he started to run once again.

★　★　★

Margaret's anxieties about Jim were mounting. He was becoming increasingly withdrawn into himself, and liable to lose his temper over the smallest thing. The evenings were the worst, after the children had gone to bed and they sat alone. Jim had taken to the radio, but he fretted over it, moving the dial back and forth. Hilversum, Athlone, Luxembourg: it was as though he were seeking a world, not just something to listen to. Whistle and static pierced the air, snatches of foreign voices and bursts of music. It was difficult for Margaret to concentrate.

'Jim, let's talk,' she said.

He looked up and switched off the radio, and Margaret laid down her book. There was no settee in the room, and they sat opposite each other in upright chairs.

'What shall we talk about?' said Jim.

'I don't know. Anything. We don't seem to talk at all these days.'

He sighed. 'I'm sorry, Maggie,' he said. 'I'm not myself.'

Margaret gazed at him, suddenly afraid of what she wanted to say.

'I understand how hard this is for you,' she began. 'But I don't think you're going about things in the best way.'

'How do you mean?'

'I mean you're feeling sorry for yourself, and that can't lead anywhere.'

Jim picked up the radio again and toyed with it. 'I've a bloody right to feel sorry for myself,' he said.

'No, Jim, you haven't. Things have happened, and we all have to deal with them as best we can.'

'I *am* trying my best.' Jim looked at her peevishly. He was so like Billy when he was in this sort of mood, she thought, so easily hurt.

'I know you are,' she said. 'But don't you think it would be better if you shared things with me?'

He put down the radio again, and looked at his hands in the way he always did when he was at a loss.

'I sometimes think I don't know how,' he said.

Margaret felt suddenly overwhelmed by her tenderness for him. She stepped over and perched on the arm of his chair.

'Let's go to bed,' she said.

Margaret undressed while he was in the bathroom, leaving her nightgown on the chair. When Jim got into bed they embraced stiffly. He began to caress her, to kiss her neck and her breasts. The flush of arousal was strange to her. She felt Jim's fingers describe a circle around her navel and descend to her thighs. He touched her, gently at first and then firmly. And then suddenly he broke away.

'I'm sorry, Maggie,' he said. 'I suppose I'm not in the mood.'

She put her arms around his neck and pressed herself to him, but he shook her off and turned over. While his body was unresponsive, hers was jangling with desire and frustration. Burying her face in the pillow, she cried as soundlessly as she could.

4

Winter closed in, and with it the margins of their life. It rained incessantly, and the farmyard became a sea of mud. The only warm rooms in the cottage were the kitchen and, when they lit a fire, the parlour. In the evenings Jim and Margaret would occupy the two armchairs while Billy and Sarah read or played games on the kitchen table. Billy had decided they should all play Monopoly, and in preparation had been trying to explain the rules to Sarah.

'The only way to learn properly is to play it,' said Jim as he sat listening to Sarah's insistent questions.

'So let's play now,' said Billy.

'It's late,' said Margaret. 'Monopoly takes ages. We'll play at the weekend if the weather hasn't changed.'

The weather didn't change, and Saturday morning was as dismal as any of the previous days. After breakfast Billy got out the Monopoly set, and began methodically to set it up.

'Dad, you must be banker,' he said.

'All right,' said Jim, laying aside yesterday's paper.

'What do you want to be, Sarah?'

'I want to be me.'

'I mean what token do you want to play with?'

'Oh.' She looked at the shiny silver tokens. 'I want the boot,' she said.

'And I want the racing car,' said Billy.

Jim took the top hat and Margaret the thimble. Sarah threw the dice first, and landed on Euston Road.

'Do you want to buy it?' said Jim.

'How much is it?'

'It says on the board. One hundred pounds.'

Sarah counted the money she'd been given. 'Yes, I will buy it,' she said. She handed Jim a hundred-pound note, and Jim gave her the card with its pale blue edge.

'You can charge me rent if I land there,' said Billy. 'Six pounds. And lots more if you get The Angel and Pentonville Road.'

'I want The Angel too,' said Sarah. 'It's a nice name.'

When she landed a fifty-pound doctor's fee she protested loudly. 'We didn't pay to go to the doctor when I had my firework burn,' she said.

'It's a game, Sarah,' said Billy. 'It's not meant to be real.'

'Come on, pay up,' said Jim.

115

Sarah tossed over a fifty-pound note, which Jim carefully banked. Billy looked across to the window. The rain streamed down the panes, and he could see no further than the other side of the yard.

'I'll swap you Oxford Street for Park Lane,' said Jim after a while. 'Plus seventy-five pounds.'

Billy looked at the dark blue card in front of him. They had driven along Park Lane on the way to the bookshop, and then into Oxford Street. This reminder made him shiver suddenly.

'I paid fifty more in the first place,' he said. 'You'll have to give me a lot more than that.'

'A hundred, then.'

'No.' Billy folded his arms and looked staunchly at his father.

'It isn't worth much to you without Mayfair,' said Jim.

'And Mayfair isn't worth much to you without Park Lane.'

'Come on, Billy, we need to move the game along. There's no point in playing unless we can start to buy houses and hotels.'

'So sell me Mayfair.'

'It's not for sale,' said Jim, and he threw the dice for his next move.

When it came to Sarah's turn she landed on Go To Jail. Billy took her boot and dumped it on the orange Jail square.

'I don't want to go to Jail,' she said. 'I haven't done anything wrong.'

'Well you have to,' said Billy. 'Those are the rules.'

'I am *not* going to Jail!'

'Yes you are. Anyway, you're already in it.'

Sarah took her boot and placed it on Water Works, which no one had yet bought.

'Sarah,' said Margaret, 'you have to play by the rules. Now put it back in Jail.'

'No I won't.' Sarah jiggled in her chair, swinging her legs rapidly back and forth.

'Then you can't play,' said Billy. 'We'll split up your properties and play without you.'

'Oh no you won't,' said Sarah, and she reached out and swept away the houses Billy had placed on Whitehall and Pall Mall. Billy stooped to pick them up from the floor.

'That's it,' he said flatly. 'You're disqualified. Isn't she, Dad?'

Jim took Sarah's hand. 'If you don't want to play, then go and read your comic,' he said. 'If you do want to play, you must go to Jail.'

Sarah slid off her chair, seized her Bunty comic, and ran up the stairs without a word. Margaret and Jim looked at one another, and Jim shrugged his shoulders.

'Let's carry on,' he said.

'I think I'll hand in my properties too,' said

Margaret. 'You two play on.'

'But it'll be no fun then,' said Billy. 'I thought we were doing it together.'

Jim looked at his watch. 'It's already taken most of the morning,' he said. 'Let's pack it up.'

Billy placed all the pieces back in the box with an air of silent protest. When he entered the bedroom Sarah buried her head in her comic and ignored him. He opened the cupboard door, and a Dinky toy Land Rover fell to the floor. As he was putting it back among the other toys, he noticed that his racing-car and sports-car sets weren't there. He ran down the stairs to tell his mother.

'They must be there,' said Margaret. 'Where else could they be?'

'They're not,' said Billy. 'I don't know where they are.'

'When did you last play with them?'

'A long time ago, with Dad. When we did the British Grand Prix.'

'Jim,' said Margaret, 'have you seen them?'

Jim laid down his paper and stared blankly into space.

'I sold them,' he said finally.

'You sold them!,' said Billy. 'But they were mine.'

'What on earth are you talking about?' said Margaret. 'You had no right at all to do that.'

Jim stood up and faced her. 'He's grown out of them,' he said. 'And we need money for food and clothes.'

'If we need money then you must say so. How could you sell Billy's toys without telling him?'

'For God's sake, Maggie,' said Jim angrily. 'Here I am doing my best to support you, and all you can do is criticize me. I've just about had it, I can tell you.'

'And so have I,' said Margaret. Abruptly she got her coat and scarf from the rack and opened the door. Rain billowed into the kitchen.

'Where are you going?' said Jim.

'For a walk.'

'It's pouring out there.'

'I couldn't care less.'

Margaret tied the scarf tightly around her head. 'You can get your own lunch,' she said, ducking out into the yard.

★ ★ ★

Billy lay on the bed and stared up at the ceiling. Sarah glanced over towards him and then returned to her comic, sneezing loudly and wrapping herself in the eiderdown. Billy looked around the tiny room. Sometimes this house felt like a prison.

'Mum's gone out into the rain,' he said.

Sarah sat up and stared at him.

'Where's she gone?'

'I don't know. For a walk.'

'Why has she gone for a walk?'

'She's cross with Dad.'

'Why?'

'Because he sold my Dinky cars.'

'He did?' said Sarah breathlessly. She looked at the teddy bear that sat on her pillow. 'He wouldn't sell my toys, would he?'

'I don't know. I don't know what he'd do.'

Billy hopped off the bed and went over to the cupboard. He searched through its contents thoroughly.

'Nothing else seems to have gone,' he said.

'Why did Daddy sell your Dinkys?'

'To buy food and clothes, so he said.'

Sarah gazed out of the window and into the gloom. Billy looked at her and saw that tears were beginning to roll down her cheeks.

'Do you think they still love each other, Mummy and Daddy?' she said.

'I think so.' He stepped across to Sarah and put his arm awkwardly around her shoulders. 'Don't worry, things will be all right when she gets back.'

'But what if she doesn't come back?'

Billy looked at his sister, at her tear-stained cheeks. There was fear in her eyes.

'I wish we hadn't come here,' she said. She sat stiffly, not leaning towards Billy, and he took his arm away.

'It's all right,' he said. 'This is just a horrible day.'

'Mummy will come back, won't she?'

'Of course she will.'

He looked across the narrow room towards the landing. But what if she doesn't come back, he said to himself, and we're left with just Dad? He thought of Jim sitting alone downstairs. How could he have sold his Dinky toys without telling him? Suddenly he knew he must talk to him.

Jim was sitting at the kitchen table smoking.

'I hadn't grown out of them,' said Billy.

Jim stubbed out his cigarette violently. 'Yes you had,' he said. 'Remember the last time? You messed it up.'

'I hadn't grown out of them,' said Billy, trying to keep his voice steady. 'And they were mine.'

'Who paid for them?'

'But you gave them to me.'

'Don't you lecture me, my boy. Wait until you find out what it's like to try and make your way in this world.'

Billy stared at his father, who carried on pressing the stub of his cigarette into the ashtray even though it was long extinguished, and then turned and ran upstairs again. Back in the bedroom he pulled his copy of *Robinson Crusoe* from the shelf and lay down on the floor. He had got to the place where Crusoe first meets Man Friday. Flipping back the pages to when Crusoe was still alone, he began to read.

★　★　★

Margaret's headscarf was no protection against the rain, and by the time she had gone a few hundred yards she was soaked. She was furious with Jim; he seemed to have lost his bearings completely. She pressed on, and it was only when Tanyard Cottage came into sight that it occurred to her to call on Leonora Vale.

'What on earth are you doing out in this weather, poppet?' she said as she opened the door.

'I just wanted to get away for a bit, that's all.'

'Come in, come in this instant.'

She gave Margaret a towel and went to put the kettle on. Margaret dried her hair and face, and accepted a mug of tea laced once again with the contents of the hip flask.

'That'll take care of you.'

'I'm sorry, Miss Vale,' said Margaret. 'I think I'm becoming a burden to you.'

'Nonsense. And you must call me Leonora. Now what's going on?'

Margaret gave her a guarded account of the morning's events, without directly referring to Jim's having sold the Dinky toys.

'You're cramped in that cottage,' said Leonora. 'You need more space. You in particular. You're letting your own life revolve entirely around theirs.'

'I thought that was what was expected of me.'

'What's expected is one thing,' said Leonora, with a dismissive wave of her hand. 'What's for the best is usually quite another.'

'I was brought up to think that doing what was expected of me would make me happy.'

'We all were. That doesn't mean we can't reach some conclusions of our own.'

Margaret gripped her mug tightly. The air in the house was as fusty as ever, but somehow she didn't mind as much now.

'Tell me about yourself,' said Leonora.

Margaret shrugged. 'There isn't much to tell,' she said.

'Then tell me a little.'

Margaret leaned back into the settee.

'Well, I was born and brought up in Bath,' she said. 'My father ran an insurance business. I was in the Land Army during the war, not far from here, near Midsomer Norton. And I went to work in my father's office when the war was over, as a secretary and receptionist.'

'And then you waited for Jim,' said Leonora dryly.

'And then I waited for Jim. We met at a motor-trade dance. He was the most handsome man I'd ever seen. It was completely obvious from the beginning that we would get married. I'm not sure it ever occurred to me to say no.'

'And soon you became a mother.'

'Very soon. And for a few years that was quite enough. Jim started to do well, started to expand the business, and we moved into a large house. The children, the house, Jim's friends, the Rotary Club: that was my life.'

'Well, it was someone's life.'

'Yes. I wonder who she was?'

'You must do something of your own, something that has nothing to do with anyone else.'

'And what might that be?'

'Well, I've already said that I see an artist in you.'

Margaret looked down at her damp shoes and stockings. 'It's one thing to say you're an artist, and quite another to be one.'

'So be one.'

'Leonora, you are very kind, but I simply wouldn't know where to begin. I love reading. It's my great solace. But I could no more write than I could fly to the moon.'

'I don't think you can be sure about that.'

'I feel it.'

Leonora gazed at her for a few moments. 'I've always had trouble with my eyes,' she said. 'Would you read to me?'

'Of course, gladly. What would you like me to read?'

'What are you reading at the moment?'

'I'm about to start *Tess of the D'Urbervilles*.'

'Will you come here and read it aloud to me?'

⋆　⋆　⋆

Jim hadn't set eyes on Liz for nearly two weeks. He dropped by Goody's one day at lunchtime and asked her to have a drink that evening, and they met in the Anchor.

She was looking very lovely. He reached over and kissed her, but she pushed him away.

'Not here,' she said.

'I've missed you,' said Jim.

'I haven't been very far away. You could

125

easily have come by.'

'It's been a difficult time,' he said.

'And not just for you. If a girl's just a one-night stand she'd like to know.'

'This is not a one-night stand, Liz,' he said, putting his arm around her. 'But there are problems, problems we've both known about from the beginning. Like where to go tonight. I suppose your parents are around?'

'Yes,' she said. She looked away, and then turned back and kissed him gently on the lips. 'I'm sorry.'

They sat quietly, holding hands under the table. I've got to work something out, Jim thought, got to find a place we can go. This is like being seventeen again.

He went up to order another round of drinks, and at that moment Gordon Towker walked in. He saw Jim and joined him at the bar.

'Can I buy you a drink?' he said.

Jim nodded over his shoulder. 'I'm with someone, thanks anyway.'

Towker's gaze followed Jim's, and he smiled nastily. 'Wouldn't want to barge in on the lovebirds,' he said.

'Another time, then.'

Jim picked up his beer and Liz's glass of wine and returned to his seat.

'Cheers,' he said.

126

'So you know him?' said Liz.

'Gordon Towker? He sort of picked me up in the Star.'

'You want to be careful with that man.' She looked across at him disapprovingly.

'Do I?'

'Yes. He's a strange one.'

'Strange how?'

She hesitated, sipping her wine. 'Well, for a start he was caught behind the swimming baths with a boy from the Blue School a while ago.'

Christ, thought Jim. 'What happened?' he said.

'Nothing. It was all hushed up.'

'Anything else I should know about him?'

Liz looked towards Towker again. It was clear that he knew he was being talked about.

'He's a bad lot, that's all,' she said.

Jim looked down at his hands. 'Let's change the subject,' he said. 'What's on at the pictures? We could go one day soon.'

'*A Town Like Alice*, I think it's called.'

'I know. It's set in Malaya during the war.'

She looked out across the dark, smoky room. 'Malaya,' she said. 'Sunshine. I could use some of that.'

He took a draught of beer. 'Shall we go somewhere else?' he said.

'Such as?'

Jim looked out of the window across Market Place. It was a bitter night. He thought of the set of keys Reg had recently given him.

'Let's go to the shop,' he said.

'To the shop?'

'Have you got a better idea?'

'And make a cosy nest out of school uniforms?'

Jim kissed her hard on the mouth. 'I want you, Liz,' he said.

She looked at him coolly. 'I'm not coming into Underhill's with you,' she said, and she stood up and began to put on her coat.

'Sit down, sweetheart.'

'I'm going home.' Her lips were pressed together, her eyes narrowed.

'Don't be angry, I'm only doing my best.'

'I'm not angry. I just want to be treated like a lady, that's all.'

She turned away from him and crossed to the door. Jim was intensely aware of Towker's having witnessed this scene. He stood up too quickly, knocking over the table and spilling the remains of their drinks. For a moment he thought to pick up the glasses, but instead he marched across the pub and out into the street. An icy wind was blowing, and Liz was nowhere in sight.

Alan had told Billy he was joining the Scouts, and Jim agreed that Billy could go along to the meeting to see whether he might want to join too. Everything was hushed in the cold night as they walked towards Walton. The Scout troop met in a wooden hut just off the main road. The Scoutmaster was a tall, slightly stooped man with a straggly moustache and a weak chin. Billy thought he looked ridiculous in his shorts and long socks held up by green garters.

'Welcome to the Walton troop, Tyler,' he said to Billy. 'This evening you will be sworn in as a tenderfoot.' He looked from Billy to Alan. 'And I hope your friend will be inspired to join us too.'

'He's Tyler,' said Billy, pointing to Alan. 'I'm Palmer.'

'Of course you are,' said the Scoutmaster. 'And I'm Wilkins. But you call me Scout-master, because that's what I am.'

The hut was very small. A single-bar electric fire gave out a faint heat, and a trestle-table stood on the bare floor, the Union Flag behind it. There were ten Scouts, ranging in age from eleven to fourteen or so, none of whom Billy knew. They seemed very sure of themselves, very pleased to be wearing their scarves and hats and badges. At a command from the Scoutmaster they formed two lines.

'Tyler,' said the Scoutmaster to Billy, 'you will join the Owl patrol. And Palmer, you can too, for this evening.'

Alan and Billy stood alongside the boys of Owl patrol, facing the Raven patrol on the other side.

'Scouts,' said the Scoutmaster sonorously. 'We will commence with the swearing in of the new boy. Come here, Tyler.'

Alan stepped forward, and the Scoutmaster looked from him to Billy for a moment. 'Yes, of course,' he said. 'Tyler.' He looked down the ranks of the two patrols. 'What do we ask a new Scout to swear to?'

In unison the boys said, 'To be loyal to God and the Queen, to help other people at all times, and to obey the Scout law.'

'Good,' said the Scoutmaster. 'Now, do you swear those things, Tyler?'

'What's the Scout law?' said Alan.

'We'll get to that later. Now do you swear?'

A titter went around the other boys.

'I swear,' said Alan.

'Good. Do you know the motto of the Scouts?'

'Yes,' said Alan. 'Be prepared.'

'And do you know the significance of those words?'

'Well, you have to be prepared in case of danger and that.'

'And what else has the initials B. P.?'

Alan thought for a moment. 'The petrol company,' he said.

'No, no,' said the Scoutmaster irritably. 'Baden-Powell. You know who he was, don't you?'

'He was the founder of the Scouts.'

'Quite right. The hero of Mafeking. Now, we will sing the Scout's Chorus. Ready?'

The boys held their breath for a moment, and then on a signal from the Scoutmaster the two patrol-leaders began to sing 'Een gonyâma, gonyâma!', to which the others responded with 'Invooboo. Yah bô! Yah bô! Invooboo.'

Alan turned to look at Billy, a sly smile forming around his mouth. Billy suppressed a smile of his own, and stood up straight.

'I expect you're wondering what that means, Tyler,' said the Scoutmaster.

'Yes, sir.'

'It means 'He is a lion!' and 'He is better than that. He is a hippopotamus!' '

'Why is a hippopotamus better than a lion?'

'Have you read Kipling?'

'No.'

'Read Kipling. Read *Kim*. Then you'll know.'

'Can we do Kim's game?' said the patrol-leader of the Owl patrol.

'Very well. Where are the things?'

There was a rush to a box under the trestle-table. 'I have to put them out,' said the Scoutmaster. 'You lot aren't allowed to see them.' He produced a tray, and then set out on it a number of small articles. Billy could see a button, a pencil, a cork, a walnut, and a couple of rags. The Scoutmaster made a show of hiding them under a cloth. Then he turned to the Scouts, taking a pencil and a piece of paper from his shirt pocket.

'I'm going to take away the cloth for one minute,' he said. 'You must try to memorize as many of these things as you can. I will then ask you to step up one at a time and whisper to me all the things you can remember.'

He whisked away the cloth, and the boys gathered around and peered at the tray. Billy's view was obscured by boys standing in front of him, but he was able to see about ten of the things, and he began to repeat to himself what they were. There followed a laborious process in which each of the boys went up to the Scoutmaster, who noted down their names and the things they had remembered. By the time it came to Billy's turn he had forgotten most of them.

'This is a silly game,' he said to Alan as he went back into line. 'If they've played it before, the others will remember what the things are anyway.'

The winner was the patrol-leader of Raven patrol. The Scoutmaster congratulated him. 'You must all learn to be observant,' he said. 'It's the most important thing.'

Billy leaned towards Alan. 'I thought being prepared was the most important thing,' he said.

'I don't think he knows what he's talking about.'

The boy next to them elbowed Alan hard. 'Shut up,' he said. 'Do you want to be a Scout or don't you?'

They listened quietly to the Scoutmaster telling them a long and involved story about how a shepherd boy in the north somewhere had lured a murderer to his arrest, and ended with the Scout War Dance, in which the boys stepped forward and back and around in circles, all the while shouting the chorus they had sung earlier. Billy found it quite baffling, and was glad when it was over.

As they walked back through the dark towards home, Alan kicked a stone into the ditch and said, 'I don't think I want to be in the Scouts after all.'

'Nor do I,' said Billy, and they smiled at one another broadly.

★　★　★

The shop was dark and empty when Jim arrived. It was unlike Reg not to be there before him, and he wasn't sure for a moment what to do. He decided he had better open up. His keys were to the shop itself, but not to the office or the safe. He switched on the lights, turned the sign to 'open', and took up his place behind the counter. Ten minutes later the phone rang, but he was unable to get into the office to answer it. Something was wrong with all this. After a while the door opened, and Norman Elsworth from Herring's China Shop stepped inside. His movements were slow, his expression grave.

'Reg has had a stroke,' he said.

Jim slumped down on the stool by the till.

'Is it bad?' he said.

Elsworth nodded in response.

'Where is he?'

'In the Infirmary. Winnie's with him. She says she'll be by as soon as she can.'

'I'm sorry,' said Jim, staring across the room.

'So am I.'

After Elsworth had left, Jim took in the

sombre aspect of the shop as though for the first time. He was stunned, quite unable to think things through. When Winifred arrived he stared at her, words failing him.

'How is he?' he said at last.

'He's unconscious,' she replied. 'He doesn't know yet what's happened.' She looked pale and exhausted.

'How bad is it?'

'They don't know yet. But at the very least he's not going to be able to come back here for a while.'

He tried to give her a hug, but the difference in their heights made it a clumsy gesture.

'I'm so sorry, Winnie,' he said.

'He'll be all right,' she said hollowly. 'Once I get him back home he'll be all right.'

'When can I visit him?'

'Not today. I'll let you know.'

They opened up the office, and Jim put change in the till. He passed the hours in a daze. He felt he should tell the customers about Reg, and several of them seemed to forget what it was they had come for and simply gave him their condolences. At half past five he shut up shop and put the takings into the night safe at the bank. As he cycled home he tried to think about the consequences of all this, but his thoughts strayed haphazardly. When Margaret asked him what might happen to the shop, he could answer only that he had no idea.

Winifred phoned him the next morning and told him that Reg was able to receive visitors.

'He won't be able to talk, though,' she said. 'He's going to need speech therapy before he can do that again.'

Jim hesitated, and then said, 'We should have a word about the shop, Winnie.'

'Yes. I'll come by tomorrow.'

The Infirmary stood back from the Glastonbury road, a large Victorian building with Gothic flourishes that made it look almost like a church. Jim hated hospitals, hated the odours of sickness and its cures, the echoing sounds of footsteps and the banging of doors. He'd had mercifully few occasions to step inside one except for when the children had been born, and even then he had felt an urge to get away as quickly as possible. A nurse directed him to Reg's ward. It was a large, green room with a dozen or so beds in it. Their occupants stared bleakly at this handsome man who would soon be able to turn around and go home.

The nurse had warned Jim that Reg would be practically unable to respond to him, and Jim wanted simply to register his presence and go. Reg lay quite inert, an oxygen mask over his nose and mouth. A faint sign of recognition showed in his eyes as Jim sat down next to the bed.

'Hello, Reg,' he said.

Reg nodded, and Jim wrestled with his unwillingness to say the obvious things.

'Comfortable, are you?'

Reg nodded again, and a strange, soft grunt came from beneath the mask.

'They'll have you out of here in no time, won't they?'

Reg turned to look away down the length of the ward. This is hopeless, thought Jim.

'I'll come back when you've got that bloody mask off,' he said. 'You look like Dan Dare.'

Jim thought he detected a hint of a smile, or perhaps it was a grimace. Reg's eyes had never smiled, only his mouth.

'Don't worry about the shop,' he said. Reg didn't respond, and he felt a sudden wave of anger pass over him. The cranky bastard had this coming, he thought, and he's left me high and dry. He made his apologies and left. In the frigid air outside he collected his bicycle from the shed and pushed out onto the road.

★   ★   ★

Winifred came by the shop the next morning. Jim made a cup of tea, and they sat on the hard chairs in the office, Jim listening out for the entrance of customers.

'He's paralysed down his left side,' said Winifred.

'Christ,' muttered Jim, and then, 'sorry, Winnie.'

She reached out and laid her hand on his. 'It's all right: that's exactly what I'd like to say.'

'Will he make a full recovery?'

Winifred shook her head. 'Nothing like,' she said. She looked around the cluttered room. 'He won't be coming back here, not ever.'

'What will you do?' he said.

'Well, I can either sell up or ask you to take it over.'

'Me?' he said, a note of alarm in his voice.

'Who else?'

'But I wouldn't know where to begin.'

'Of course you would. You've been working here for nearly three months now.'

'Winnie, with respect, Reg hardly involved me at all. I know nothing about buying stock and such things.'

She looked at him thoughtfully for a moment. 'It's up to you, Jim,' she said. 'If you want to take it over, then we'll agree on a salary and I'll do all I can to help. Otherwise I'm bound to sell the place, and there's no certainty that a buyer would want to keep you on.'

Jim stood up and scratched the back of his neck. He looked around him, from the dingy office to the stockroom and out into the deserted shop, and then back at Winifred.

'I'll have to think it over,' he said. 'You can rely on me to take care of the place for a while, at any rate.'

Winifred stood and gave him a peck on the cheek. 'Ring me on Monday,' she said.

She made to collect her things, and Jim held out her coat. She slipped her arms into it, buttoned it up, and smoothed down the lapels. 'Do think about it, Jim,' she said. 'And think about Margaret and the children.'

After she had gone, he stood disconsolately behind the counter. The empty gabardines and suits hung from their rails, mocking him. He had never felt so trapped in his life.

★ ★ ★

At the end of the school day Miss Shute asked Billy, Alan, Frank and two of the girls to stay behind. She sat them in the desks at the front.

'Next term you will all be taking your

eleven-plus exam,' she said. 'I hope you understand what that means.'

'It's to see if we can go to grammar school,' said Audrey Purchase.

'That's right. If you pass you will go to the Blue School in Wells, which is a very old and very fine school.'

'And if we don't pass?' said Alan.

'Then you will go to the secondary modern school, which is also a fine school, but not as fine as the Blue School.'

'What will we have to do?' said Billy.

'We are going to have to do a little of everything,' said Miss Shute. 'At the beginning of term I will show you an old exam paper, so that you can see the sort of questions you'll be given. There will be reading, writing, arithmetic, science and art. Some children have to do French too, but you're excused that.'

'I'd like to learn French, miss,' said Billy.

'You'll do so if you go to the Blue School, Billy, as I'm sure you will. But we are going to have to work hard next term, do you understand?'

Billy and Alan and Frank started walking home together. At the crossroads where Frank turned up the hill they stood for a few moments in a knot.

'I couldn't care less about the eleven-plus,'

said Frank. 'My dad says the secondary school is good enough for anyone.'

'It depends what you want to do when you grow up,' said Billy.

'That's easy. I'm going to take over the farm.'

'What are you going to do, Billy?' said Alan.

He stood thinking for a moment. 'I'm going to be an explorer,' he said finally.

'And explore what?' said Frank.

'I don't know. I bet there are places in Africa and South America that haven't been explored.'

'Yeah, places not worth exploring,' said Frank. 'With lots of snakes and bugs.'

'I'll be an archaeologist, then.'

'A what?'

'An archaeologist. Someone who finds old forts and towns and things, under the ground.'

'Like the bloke who found the mummies,' said Alan.

'What mummies?' said Frank.

'You know, in Egypt. That king, Toot somebody.'

'He was cursed,' said Billy. 'The curse of the mummies.'

'What happened to him?' said Frank.

'He died.'

'Well of course he died. But how?'

'I think he was poisoned,' said Alan. 'That was the curse.'

'I'm not bloody well going to get poisoned,' said Frank. 'I'm going to stay where I belong.'

'Well I don't belong anywhere,' said Billy. 'So I'm going to explore and find things.' He began to run along the road towards Coombe, and then turned around. 'Are you coming?' he said. Alan shrugged his shoulders and made to follow him.

'You don't need to go to any school, then,' shouted Frank. 'You just need to get lost.'

*   *   *

Billy was going to be an explorer and an archaeologist. He hadn't understood this until the conversation with Frank and Alan, but now his conviction was unshakeable. He began to devour adventure stories set in faraway places. Through school or the mobile library he got hold of Rider Haggard's *King Solomon's Mines*, John Buchan's *Prester John*, Conan Doyle's *The Lost World*. He spent the long winter evenings lying on the floor by the fire, his imagination taking flight. When he went out walking through the fields he was no longer in Somerset but on the veld in South Africa. The stream that ran by the school was the Amazon. And the tor was Everest, the most challenging mountain in the world. At night he lay in bed listening to the sounds of Sarah's gentle breathing and inventing stories of his own, stories in which he was always the hero. And it was into this vivid world that new and strange sensations began to enter.

It had begun one morning, when he awoke to find that his penis was quite stiff. He touched it cautiously, but at that moment his mother called him to come down for breakfast. The stiffness quickly passed. When it happened again in the evening, as he lay waiting for sleep, it seemed even more strange and exciting. It must have something to do with all these daydreams, he thought. And over the next few nights, he found he could summon this change by thinking of mountains and waterfalls and jungles. The more he touched himself the nicer were the feelings he could bring on, until one night he simply couldn't stop, and after a while he experienced a strong tingling sensation, followed by a sense of happiness that stayed with him until he drifted into sleep.

This was a most extraordinary thing. Why hadn't anyone told him about it? Every night now he went through this secret ritual, and it seemed to him that every night it became more enjoyable, more comforting. But what was it? There was only one person he could ask.

Billy called at the Tyler farm the next morning, and he and Alan set off into the woods. They arrived at the place they had come to the first time they had been together, and sat down on the damp earth, gazing at the horizon.

'Alan,' said Billy. 'Are you having strange feelings?'

'What sort of strange feelings?'

'In your willy. Is it going stiff sometimes?'

Alan smirked. 'Sure,' he said. 'I've had them for a while.'

'So what happens?'

'I have a wank.'

'A wank?'

'Yeah, I give it a pull.'

Billy let out a sigh of relief. 'So do I,' he said.

'Everyone does,' said Alan. 'Frank even had a wanking circle at his place once, when his parents were out.'

'A circle?'

'Four of us sat on the floor in his room and pulled on our willies. Frank's got spunk, too.'

'What's spunk?'

'It's the sticky white stuff that makes

babies. You know, the seed. We'll get it soon, I reckon.'

'It makes babies? How?'

Alan looked at Billy pityingly. 'Hasn't your dad told you the facts of life?' he said.

'No.'

'Well ask him. My dad told me ages ago. He tried to keep a straight face, but he couldn't.'

'So what did he say?'

'He said how babies are made. How you put your willy inside a girl.'

'Inside a girl?'

''Course. Then the spunk goes inside her tummy and makes a baby. It's like the cows and the pigs. You must have seen them doing it.'

Billy had never heard anything so improbable in his life. He thought of Sarah, of the little fold of skin that she peed out of. Was that where you put it? He gazed out across the countryside and wondered how he could find a way of asking his father. But no, he would ask his mother first.

That night as Billy lay in bed he thought of Sarah, and of Audrey at school, but he still couldn't make a connection between girls and these feelings he now so easily aroused. He thought instead of clouds scudding across a blue sky. And he thought that perhaps he wouldn't talk to his mother about this just yet.

★ ★ ★

Every few days now, Margaret would set off for Tanyard Cottage in the middle of the morning and read *Tess of the D'Urbervilles* to Leonora Vale. It was something she had come to look forward to eagerly. Leonora would sit back in her chair, a dreamy expression softening her features. Margaret hadn't considered herself a good reader, but after a few chapters she became quite fluent, hesitating or stumbling less often. And after an hour or so of reading, they would talk for a while until it was time for Margaret to go home.

Leonora seemed to Margaret to be very bound up in the destiny of Tess Durbeyfield. Margaret had forgotten how highly wrought was Hardy's language, how mystical his imagery. After a few mornings she came to the chapter in which Tess's baby is taken ill. 'Poor Sorrow's campaign against sin, the world, and the devil was doomed to be of limited brilliancy,' she read, ' — luckily perhaps for himself, considering his beginnings. In the blue of the morning that fragile soldier and servant breathed his last, and

146

when the other children awoke they cried bitterly, and begged Sissy to have another pretty baby.' She paused and looked up, and saw that tears were streaming down Leonora's cheeks.

'It's terribly sad, isn't it?' said Margaret, not sure whether to go on.

Leonora took out a handkerchief.

'My baby's name was Astraea,' she said eventually. 'She died of meningitis just before her first birthday.'

Margaret set aside the book and looked at the rumpled figure sitting across from her. Leonora suddenly seemed very small and frail.

'I'm so sorry,' said Margaret. 'I had no idea.'

'Of course you hadn't, poppet,' said Leonora, blowing her nose loudly. She paused to collect herself. 'I was quite old, especially for those days — thirty-five.' She stared beyond Margaret. 'My dancing days were over, and I had no idea what to do. A man came along, a kind man I thought, and we had a child. But Astraea never had a chance, and after she died the man left me.'

Margaret thought of Billy and Sarah, and felt a shudder go through her. The death of a child was surely the worst thing of all.

Leonora gathered herself up and smiled.

'I'll put the kettle on again,' she said. 'How foolish of me to cry over something that happened more than twenty years ago.'

'It's not foolish at all,' said Margaret. 'Now let me make the tea.'

As Margaret walked back to the house, her thoughts dwelled on Leonora. The more she learned about her the more intriguing she became. She must have lived there alone for many years. What did she do with herself all day, an intelligent woman who had difficulty reading and whose only company, besides Margaret herself and the cats, was the radio? She was wandering in the middle of the road when suddenly from around the bend a large silver car shot towards her. She leaped into the ditch and fell awkwardly, covering herself in mud. The car screeched to a halt, and two people stepped out and ran back up the hill. Margaret stood brushing away the dirt.

'My dear young lady,' said the driver. 'I'm so awfully sorry.'

He was a rakish man in a fawn camel-hair coat and shiny brown shoes.

'It's perfectly all right,' she said. 'I was jaywalking.'

'And David was going too fast,' said the woman. 'I've told him a thousand times to drive more slowly around here.'

She was about Margaret's age, and wore a

fox fur coat and an elaborate hat. Her oval face was carefully made-up. Like her companion, she seemed wholly out of place on this country road.

'May we offer you a lift?' said the man.

'That's very kind, but I live less than half a mile away, and in the wrong direction for you.'

'You live nearby?'

As he said this, it dawned on Margaret who they must be.

'At Fosse's Farm,' she said.

'Then we're neighbours. We live in Coombe Hall.' He thrust out his hand. 'David Latymer,' he said. 'This is my wife, Clare.'

They were flustering her, these sleek people. 'I had better get home and clean my coat,' she said.

'Of course,' said Latymer. 'But we must make this up to you. You must come for a drink one evening.'

'That would be very pleasant,' said Margaret, thinking that it would probably not be pleasant at all.

'What is your telephone number?'

'We're not on the phone.'

'Then we will send you a note,' said Clare. 'How nice to meet you.'

5

The car stood in the yard like a magnificent black beast. Billy soaped its haunches gently, while Jim worked on the radiator grille. Since Winifred didn't drive, she had simply handed over the keys. To all intents, the Vanguard was now theirs.

'How big an engine has it got?' asked Billy.

'It's a two-litre.'

'What's a litre?'

'It's something like two pints.'

'Like pints of milk?'

'Yes.'

Billy tried to imagine four milk bottles under the bonnet.

'Can we see?'

'When we've finished washing it.'

All Billy's scorn for this car had vanished the moment his father drove it home. It was a car and it was theirs, and that was all that mattered. Jim splashed a bucket of water over the roof, and they shammied it dry. It shone brightly in the cold sunlight.

Jim opened up the bonnet and they looked inside. Strangely, Billy had never seen a car engine before, nor wondered what it might be like. His father was more interested in the lines of a car than its innards. The engine and the other mechanisms were weirdly complicated, pipes and wires and rubber tubes sprouting everywhere like the stems of an exotic plant.

'These are the four cylinders,' said Jim.

'The four pints.'

'That's right. The Jaguar had eight. Here's where you put in the oil, and that thing there is the windscreen washer refill.'

'What's this?' said Billy, pointing to a bulbous contraption with a stopper at its head.

'I think that's for the brake fluid.'

Jim closed the bonnet and brushed his hands on his trousers. 'She's all right, this one,' he said. He patted the car's front wing, and they stood back to admire it.

'So now can we go to the tor?' said Billy.

Jim's face darkened. 'The tor?' he said. 'We'll see.'

'But why not?'

'Do you have any idea how much petrol costs?'

'No.'

'Well it's bloody expensive. Just because we've got a car again doesn't mean we can go tearing off wherever we want. The main thing is that I can drive to work and back instead of freezing on that bike.'

'But the tor isn't that far away. Surely we can afford to go just once?'

Jim picked up the bucket. 'I'll be the judge of what we can afford,' he said, and he turned towards the house.

★　★　★

It was a short step from reading aloud to Leonora Vale to auditioning at the Byre Amateur Theatrical Society, and one made possible by the car. As Margaret drove through the darkness to Wells she did her best to suppress the skittishness that had overtaken her.

The Byre Theatre was at the lower end of Chamberlain Street. As Margaret entered the foyer a very large woman appeared, holding out a hand stiffly in front of her. 'Diana Mogg,' she said loudly. 'You must be Margaret Palmer.'

She was about six feet tall, with a mane of white hair and eyes that swam behind the thick lenses of her glasses. She was both producer and director, apparently, and was a teacher at the Girls' Blue School. She led Margaret into the auditorium. Four people sitting in the front row turned and stood as they came down the aisle.

'Introductions,' said Diana Mogg. 'Michael Ford is playing Victor Prynne, Bert Dampler is Elyot Chase, Irene Beer is Louise, the maid, and Liz Burridge is Sybil Chase. This is Margaret Palmer, who we're auditioning for the part of Amanda Prynne.'

There was a general shaking of hands and nodding of heads.

'I'm sorry if this seems like an inquisition,' said Diana. 'We thought we had our Amanda, but she's moving, and has had to drop out.'

Margaret suddenly felt very vulnerable. She hadn't done anything like this since school. There was a catch in her throat, and she wished she could have a glass of water.

'We'll start with Victor and Amanda's first scene,' said Diana. 'You've read the play, I trust?'

Margaret brandished her French's acting edition of *Private Lives*. 'I can't say I'm familiar with it yet,' she said.

'Oh, never mind about that. If I give you the part, you'll soon be very familiar with it.'

Margaret and Michael Ford stepped up onto the stage, and stood awkwardly in the centre. 'Don't bother about stage directions,' said Diana. 'Just think about the words.'

Michael Ford was a good-looking young man with olive skin and very dark eyes that stared at her in a way that Margaret felt was not yet called for by the script.

'Now,' said Diana. 'You are on a hotel balcony in Deauville with your new husband. You are very rich, and you have nothing better to do than to indulge in idle chatter about whether it would be nicer to be in Paris. Your first husband, unbeknownst to you, is in the next room with his new wife, and you will soon bump into him. You are very beautiful, Margaret, and you are wearing a negligee.'

Michael laughed nervously, and then looked abruptly down at his script.

'Come on then, Victor,' said Diana.

Michael cleared his throat and spoke his first line. 'Mandy,' he said, to which Margaret replied, 'What?'

'Come outside, the view is wonderful.'

'I'm still damp from the bath. Wait a minute . . . I shall catch pneumonia, that's what I shall catch.'

Before Michael could speak his next line, Diana stood up and shouted 'Diaphragm!' Margaret looked down at her, startled by the interruption.

'Pardon?'

'Use your diaphragm. You're speaking from here,' she said, pointing to her throat, 'when you should be speaking from here.' With this she thumped her stomach very hard. 'Now go back to the beginning.'

Margaret breathed deeply and spoke her lines as clearly as she could. She had no idea how to use her diaphragm.

'God!' said Michael.

'I beg your pardon?'

'You look wonderful.'

'Thank you, darling.'

'Like a beautiful advertisement for something.'

'Nothing peculiar, I hope.'

'I can hardly believe it's true. You and I, here alone together, married!'

Margaret began to relax, and even to enjoy the banter of these frivolous characters. When they came to the end of the scene she looked down expectantly.

Diana turned to the others, paused for a moment, and said, 'I think we have our Amanda.'

Margaret heaved a sigh of relief, and Michael leaned across and kissed her on the cheek. 'Wonderful, darling,' he said.

They left the theatre and walked together to the Swan Hotel, where Michael insisted on buying the drinks. They were in ebullient mood, and only Liz Burridge seemed to Margaret to hold back.

'Now all we need is for someone to take

over from Winnie Underhill on the costumes,' said Diana.

'I might have something in my wardrobe that would do,' said Margaret, thinking of an evening dress she had managed to hold on to.

'Good,' said Diana, gazing at her almost affectionately. 'Oh, Margaret,' she said, clapping her hands, 'you *are* Amanda!'

They sat in the armchairs chatting and scheming. This was Margaret's first night out since they had come to Coombe, and she was light-headed by now.

'We must do an article on the production in the New Year,' said Michael, 'to get the ball rolling.' He turned to Margaret. 'I'm on the *Wells Journal*. Features.'

'That must be very interesting.'

'Until I land a job with one of the nationals, yes.' He smiled at her artlessly. 'I'm going places, you see.'

★ ★ ★

Margaret and Billy and Sarah drove into Wells one morning to do some shopping for Christmas presents. To Billy the deliberations over what to buy and for whom and how much seemed endless, and he was glad when it was finally over and they could go to the Bishop's Palace. They wandered across to the

156

gatehouse, and watched the ducks scoot about in the moat.

'Do you see that rope?' said Margaret. 'The swans tug on it when they're hungry, and it rings a bell.'

'How do they do that?' said Sarah.

'With their beaks.'

'Let's see them do it.'

'They don't seem to be around. We'll come back another day.'

Sarah looked crestfallen, and Margaret took her hand. They walked to the cathedral, and entered the door under the carved figures of the west face. The vaulted arches of the nave soared above them.

'This must be the biggest church in the world,' said Billy, his mouth agape as he craned to look upwards.

'One of the biggest, I'm sure.'

He stood absorbing the wonderful stillness of the place.

'Will we go to our church at Christmas?' he said.

'Would you like to?'

'Yes. It's Jesus's birthday. We went last Christmas, didn't we?'

Margaret gazed towards the quire without replying. She had never been in the least religious, but a place like this was a challenge to her unbelief. After a few moments she said,

'I need a cup of coffee before we go home. Would you two like a lemonade?'

They walked across the green, along Sadler Street and into Goody's café. The place was full of people, and very stuffy. The waitress seemed to recognize Margaret.

'This is Liz Burridge,' she said to the children. 'She's in the play with me.'

Liz smiled shyly without saying anything, and took their order. When she returned she spilled coffee into the saucer, and this seemed to distress her far more than it should have done. She fussed over it with a cloth.

'I'm so clumsy,' she said.

When she was out of earshot, Margaret said, 'She's a strange girl, that one. Goodness knows how she's going to carry off the part of Sybil.'

'Who's Sybil?' said Billy.

'She's a character in my play. She's a very chatty character.'

'She doesn't look very chatty to me.'

★ ★ ★

Jim found himself settling into his new routines. Winifred Underhill had been a great help at first, but now that Reg was back at home, she left Jim to his own devices. He quickly realized that running the shop was essentially no different from running the car showroom. Reg had been meticulous in his record-keeping, and it wasn't hard to work out who to speak to about what. While he reproached himself for it continually, Jim couldn't help but feel relieved at having the place to himself. He thought about taking on a junior, but decided it wasn't necessary provided his customers knew not to call at lunchtime. He still felt confined much of the time, but he told himself there was nothing to be done about that.

He had seen Liz once since the evening in the Anchor, and it had been strained. She had got him to promise that now that he had the use of a car, they would take a trip somewhere soon; but one way or another he hadn't set a date.

Since he could afford a shepherd's pie or a bowl of soup for lunch these days, he had taken to going to the Crown. One day as he was finishing off his pint of beer he glanced at a copy of the *Wells Journal* belonging to someone at the next table. The headline read, 'Three Wells Men Arrested for Book Theft'.

He quickly left the pub and bought a copy of the paper. Back in the shop he sat down and read the story.

'Three local men, and a bookseller in London, were arrested this week on charges of theft and receiving stolen goods. George Crocker and Arthur Trafford were charged with stealing a large number of antique books from the house of Mr Alfred Pettigrew, owner of Pettigrew's Printing Works. Gordon Towker, another local man, and Bernard Smith, a bookseller with premises near the British Museum, were charged with receiving stolen goods.

'Mr Pettigrew's house was broken into on the night of the 21st of September. Wells Police believe that Crocker and Trafford took away as many as thirty books, valued at more than a thousand pounds. It is alleged that Towker then took receipt of them and sold them on to Mr Smith. Police from the Theobalds Road station in west central London arrested Smith after an anonymous buyer reported his suspicion that a book Smith attempted to sell him came from Mr Pettigrew's collection. It would appear that Smith gave the police Towker's name, and that Towker in turn gave Wells Police the names of Crocker and Trafford.

'All four men have been released on

bail, pending proceedings at Wells Assizes early in the New Year.'

Jim laid down the paper and sank back into his chair. You bloody fool, he thought. What on earth were you thinking of? He stared out into the shop, Towker's words coming back to him: 'He doesn't know your name, and he won't ask.'

Smith had clearly shopped Towker, and Towker had shopped the thieves. If Jim were going to receive a visit from the police, then surely it would have happened by now. What exactly had Towker said about how the books got to London? He looked down at his sweaty, fidgeting hands. There was nothing to do but sit it out, and stay out of Towker's way.

The bell on the front door rang, and Jim sprang up from his chair.

'Mr Palmer?' said his customer.

He couldn't have been thirty, but the top of his high domed head was quite bald except for a few sandy wisps. He had a girl's mouth and soft grey eyes.

'Winnie Underhill suggested I call by. My name's Bert Dampler. I work at the Regal. I'm in a play, *Private Lives*, and I'm going to need a suit.'

'My wife's in that play.'

'Yes, and we're very glad to have her.' He

bobbed up and down as he spoke; if he weren't so deferential, Jim might have supposed he was spoiling for a fight.

'You're going to want something that looks like it's from the thirties.' Jim went across to the rack of suits. 'None of these were made for the casino at Deauville, I'm afraid,' he said. He took down the darkest suit he could find. 'This might be a bit big for you, but no doubt we can take up the hems and sleeves.'

Dampler went into the changing room and emerged a few moments later, his feet tripping over the trouser-ends. Jim knelt down to take them up, pinning them in place.

'Put your shoes back on and take a look in the mirror,' he said.

Dampler didn't look at all bad. 'You'll need a crisp white shirt and a dicky bow. What's your character's name?'

'Elyot Chase.'

'Well, Elyot, I think you cut a fine figure. That'll be eight pounds.'

Jim took up the sleeves of the jacket and made out an alterations slip. As he was handing it to Dampler he said, 'So my wife's got a future on the stage, has she?'

'Well, we've only seen her in the audition so far. But she's perfect for the part. She's smart, your wife.'

'Yes,' said Jim. 'I suppose she is.'

Billy missed the television, and Alan had told him there were children's matinees at the Regal. Alan persuaded his father to drive them in the milk lorry to Wells one day, and they went to see *Flash Gordon*. A queue of boys waited patiently outside the cinema. They bought gobstoppers and sat in the dim light waiting for the films to start.

Billy had seen *Flash Gordon* on television, but on the cinema screen it seemed rather flimsy. Flash's rocket fizzed as it streaked towards the planet Mongo. Ming the Merciless had unleashed a deadly purple dust on the Earth, and had to be stopped. Billy watched as Flash and Dr Zarkov fought their way into Ming's palace, where the evil scientist was experimenting on his victims in a glass tube. There were four short films, by the end of which Flash had managed to save the Earth. As they stepped back into the foyer Billy said, 'That wasn't very good, was it?'

'They're old films,' said Alan. He looked at the posters advertising forthcoming attractions. 'They should have some newer stuff here.'

'There's a *Hopalong Cassidy* programme on after Christmas,' said Billy. 'It says so outside.'

'He's not much better,' said Alan.

They went out into the street, and stood wondering what to do until Alan's father returned to pick them up.

'Let's go and see the Blue School,' said Billy.

They asked someone the way, and walked along Princes Road until they came upon a weathered brick building that stood back a little from the street.

'It's red!' said Alan.

'I don't think it's called the Blue School for that reason,' said Billy.

'Maybe they see it as blue when we see it as red,' said Alan with a smile.

As they were walking back, Billy looked down a side road and saw a black Standard Vanguard parked to one side. It was exactly the same as theirs. He turned towards it, and as he came nearer he saw from the number plate that it was indeed theirs. But his father had driven to Bath that morning, saying he had some business to do. Billy signalled to Alan to stay back, and slowly approached the car. Through the rear window he could see the outlines of two heads, one of them clearly his father's. They appeared to be having an animated conversation.

After a few moments his father leaned across and kissed the other person. The kiss lasted a long time, and involved many movements of their arms and hands. Billy stood stock still, not sure what to do. As the figures disengaged, he saw that the other person was the waitress at Goody's, Liz Burridge. His father was stroking her cheek now. Billy looked at the wing mirror, and knew that if he were to stay where he was any longer then his father might see him. He turned and ran, grabbing at Alan as he passed and gesturing to him to follow.

★ ★ ★

An invitation arrived from the Latymers. Margaret was inclined not to accept it, but Jim was curious about these people, and persuaded her to go. There was no mention of the children, so Margaret asked Hubert Fosse to look in on them.

Jim pressed the button on the entryphone, and within a few seconds the gates swung open to reveal Coombe Hall. It was odd to think that this place was almost directly across the road from the farm: there was no trace of it at all from the road.

A silver Bentley stood on the gravel outside the front door. Jim took in the house and its extensive grounds and said, 'They must be millionaires.'

David Latymer appeared from behind the double doors, and stood under the portico as they approached.

'How very good to see you,' he said. He was wearing brown corduroy trousers and a yellow cashmere jumper. He shook Jim's hand and kissed Margaret's, and led them through a hallway to an enormous room at the back. Clare Latymer raised herself from a chaise longue, laying down a copy of *Country Life*. They've rehearsed this, thought Jim, this 'rich people at their leisure' act.

'A cocktail?' said David.

Jim had never been one for fancy drinks. He hesitated for a moment.

'I usually have a dry martini at this hour,' said David.

'Thank you,' said Jim, not sure whether he had any choice.

David left the room for a moment, and Margaret complimented Clare on the house.

'We found it soon after David bought the company,' she said. 'We needed somewhere for when we're not in London.' She waved her cigarette in the air, in a gesture that encompassed the entire place. The room they were in was cluttered with furniture. Above the marble fireplace a large and ornate mirror lent Jim a view of Clare's elegant back.

David returned with a tray that bore four

glasses, a bottle of gin, a bottle of white vermouth, a silver shaker and some green olives.

'The secret of a good martini is to keep everything in the fridge, even the cocktail sticks,' he said. 'That way you don't dilute it with ice.'

Jim had drunk a martini or two in London. They were lethal. Men in the City would down two or even three before lunch every day, and somehow conduct themselves through the afternoon without forfeiting either their own fortunes or those of their clients. David flourished the shaker and poured out a cloudy liquid. He then pressed two olives onto each cocktail stick and rested them against the sides of the glasses. His movements were very precise and at the same time very casual.

'Cheers!' he said when he had passed around the glasses. 'To our new neighbours.'

They sat down on the two settees, David and Clare on one and Jim and Margaret on the other. The fire crackled, and an ormolu clock above it chimed six o'clock.

'I nearly ran over your lovely wife,' said David to Jim. 'I'm extremely glad I didn't. If I may say so, my dear chap, you are a lucky man.'

Jim took a sip of his martini. It was like

being plunged into a cold bath, the chill running all the way down to the pit of his stomach. He eyed David Latymer over his glass. His thick grey hair contrasted with jet black eyebrows that arched above very pale blue eyes. He's a phoney, thought Jim. But then, weren't all rich people phoney? He reminded himself that not so long ago he too had been well off. But not like this.

'I'm lucky in some ways,' he said. He glanced over at Clare, who had hooked her legs under her in such a way as to show off her slim ankles. She had been studying him closely. They can't work us out, Jim thought. Either that or she fancies me.

'Forgive me, Jim, if I say that we know something about you. Only the sort of things one picks up here and there, of course. And having now met you, I have no doubt at all that your fortunes will change for the better before too long.'

One day perhaps, Jim thought, people won't talk to me as though I have some incurable disease.

'Tell me about your own business,' he said.

David set down his martini glass and scooped up a handful of peanuts. 'I own the cider company in Shepton, Charlton Cider,' he said.

'But you're not from around here?'

'No, no, from London. I bought the company five years ago. It wasn't doing very well in those days.'

'And now?'

'Oh, very nicely.'

Clare Latymer stood up and suggested to Margaret that she show her around the house. Jim looked at the two women, at the contrast between the artificiality of Clare and the simplicity of Margaret. I know which one I prefer, he thought.

As they left the room, David topped up Jim's glass. This stuff was beginning to befuddle him, and he would have to be careful what he said.

'So,' said David. 'What's your plan for restoring your fortunes?'

'I'm not sure I have one. I probably won't be discharged from bankruptcy for several years, and until then I'm a bit stuck.'

'All right, so you can't be a director of a company. That doesn't mean to say you can't improve your lot.'

Jim shrugged. 'I applied for any number of jobs, and as soon as I mentioned I was a bankrupt, people went quiet on me.'

'Well, that's simple prejudice, isn't it? You speculated to accumulate, and it didn't quite work out.'

'Not quite.'

'I expect you're a good salesman.'

'I used to be.'

'That's my background, sales. I could sell anything to anyone.' David leaned back into the deep cushions.

'Well, I'm selling now, in a way.'

'You want to set your sights a little higher than that though, don't you?'

'Sure I do. I haven't quite worked out how, that's all.'

A large Golden Labrador entered the room and flopped down in front of the fire. David reached down to pat its head.

'It's a seduction, isn't it, selling?' he said. 'You have to make the other person want *you*, as much as what you're selling them. And you have to start by putting yourself in their shoes.'

'Of course.'

'And you know what you must do before you can put yourself in their shoes?'

Jim thought for a moment. The gin was already going to his head.

'You have to take off your own shoes!' said David triumphantly. 'You have to forget who you are, and see who they are.'

'Yes,' said Jim vaguely.

'They're not just buying a product, they're buying a *feeling* about themselves.' There was an evangelical glint in David Latymer's eyes.

Jim was beginning to feel very uncomfortable. He put down his drink, promising himself he wouldn't touch it again, and prayed for the return of Clare and Margaret.

'I think you should come and see me some time soon, at the cider factory.'

Jim wasn't sure what he meant by this. Was he thinking of offering him a job, or simply planning to resume the lecture?

'Thank you,' he said. 'I've never seen cider being made.'

David waved his hand dismissively. 'Oh, you can see how it's made, if you like,' he said. 'But personally, I'm more interested in how it ends up down people's throats.'

By the time Clare and Margaret returned, Jim was disliking David Latymer intensely.

'What a magnificent house,' said Margaret.

'Thank you,' said David. 'It does us during the week.'

'We usually spend our weekends in town,' said Clare. 'We're only here now because David has to be at the office in Shepton early tomorrow morning.'

Jim made to get up, and reeled back into the settee. 'We ought to be going,' he said, trying to cover his embarrassment. 'We've taken up quite enough of your time.'

They walked back through the house, and under the portico he breathed in the fresh air deeply. He extended his hand to David Latymer, who shook it forcefully. He's not sober either, he thought.

'Happy Christmas,' said Clare.

'And to you,' said Margaret. She glanced at Jim. 'I think we had better get home,' she said, 'and rescue poor Hubert from the children.'

★　★　★

It was while Billy was re-enacting the battle of the Alamo in the hayshed that he came upon the bicycle. It was a bitterly cold day, far too cold to play outside. The bike was a dark green Raleigh Junior, and it looked fairly new. What was it doing there, he wondered, so hidden away? With numb hands he pulled it out from behind a bale, brushed off the hay, and swung his leg over the crossbar. It was exactly the right size for him. Scarcely able to contain his excitement, he laid it down on the ground and raced across to the house. Jim and Margaret were sitting at the kitchen table reading separate sheets of the newspaper.

'Dad, Mum!' he shouted. 'There's a bike in the hayshed!'

His father and mother glanced at one another.

'Well, young man,' said Jim, carefully

putting together the pages of the paper, 'we'd better go and investigate, hadn't we?'

Billy practically dragged him back to the hayshed. He picked up the bike, and mounted it once again.

'It seems to be a boy's bike,' said Jim, running his hand along the handlebars. 'I wonder whose it is?'

Billy looked up at him, and watched his features break into a smile.

'Happy Christmas, Billy,' he said. 'I think it's come early this year.'

'Oh, Dad! You mean it's for me?'

'Of course it's for you. It's high time you had a set of wheels.'

Out in the yard Jim said, 'The secret is to keep moving forward. If you slow down you'll fall off.' Billy got on, and Jim placed one hand on his shoulder and the other on the back of the frame. 'We'll start doing it together,' he said. 'If you feel yourself falling then jam on the brakes and put your foot out.'

They pushed off, Billy gripping the handlebars. After a few yards Jim let go, and for a moment Billy felt suddenly, terrifyingly free before he clattered to the ground, the bike skidding out from under him. He got up, brushed off his grazed hands, and stood it upright again. They repeated the manoeuvre, Jim holding on for longer, and this time Billy was able to come gently to a standstill and stay in the saddle.

'Try going down the yard,' said Jim. 'It slopes a bit.'

Billy turned the bicycle to face towards the road, and Jim set him off. He quickly gained speed, and now his only thought was to hang on. 'Brake!' shouted his father. He pulled on the brakes, but too hard, and his momentum hurled him over the handlebars and into the ditch.

Jim raced towards him. 'You bloody fool,' he said. 'I told you to brake, not upend it.'

Billy looked up at him dazedly, wondering how he could have known how hard to brake when he'd never ridden a bike before.

'Are you all right?'

'I think so,' he said.

'Well there's no blood, just a bruise on your forehead.'

His father leaned forward and inspected his face closely. Billy pulled back and pushed away his hand.

'What's the matter?' said Jim.

Anger surged through him, with this man who always took things away just as he seemed to be giving them, who always spoiled things with his petty rages. Jim's head being so close to his like this reminded Billy of two other heads, those in the car in Wells. For a moment he considered telling his father that he knew about Liz Burridge. But he thought better of it, and got unsteadily to his feet.

'Nothing's the matter,' he said finally. 'It hurts, that's all.'

★　★　★

On the last day at school before the Christmas holidays, the Misses Shute took all the children to church.

'We do this every year,' said Alan. 'It's a special service, just for us.'

A large yew tree dominated the churchyard, and here and there were the gravestones of the children's ancestors. St Peter's Church was small and neat, its grey walls glistening after a night of rain. The children took up their places in the pews in the same positions as they had in the classroom, and Billy sat near the back with Alan, Frank, Les and Ed. The air in the church was if anything colder than outside, and with every whisper from the children came the ghost of a cloud.

The Reverend Harry Hardie watched as they settled, resting his hands on the lectern and raising himself on the balls of his feet now and then.

'Welcome, children,' he said at last, 'to our school Christmas service. We shall sing some

175

hymns and carols, and we shall ask ourselves what is the meaning of Christmas.'

Billy had never set eyes on the vicar before. He had a long grey beard, a reedy voice, and a rather startled expression.

'So, children, what *is* the meaning of Christmas?'

'Presents,' murmured Alan to Billy, and Les said quite audibly, 'Dad getting drunk.' Frank elbowed Les and told him to shut up.

'Christmas was when Our Lord Jesus was born, who came into the world to save us from our sins. Now where was Jesus born?'

Four or five hands shot up, and the vicar nodded at Sarah. 'In Bethlehem,' she said.

'Quite right. But Joseph and Mary didn't live there, did they, they lived in Nazareth. Why did they have to go to Bethlehem?'

This time the only hand that went up was Frank's. Billy had never seen him volunteer an answer to anything.

'They had to pay some taxes,' he said.

'Almost right, Frank,' said the vicar. 'Very good. They had to *register* for taxes, because Joseph was born there. And what happened when they got to Bethlehem?'

Several hands went up again. 'There was no room at the inn,' said Audrey.

'There was no room anywhere. Too many people had come to the town. So they found refuge in a stall for animals. And where did they put the baby Jesus?'

'In a manger,' said Frank before anyone else could speak.

'Yes. And what is a manger?'

'It's a trough, that animals eat out of.'

Billy looked across at Frank. He was eager and attentive, quite different from the boy who sat at the back of the schoolroom doodling or throwing paper aeroplanes.

'Meanwhile,' continued the vicar, 'in the hills outside the town, there were some shepherds tending their flocks. And an angel appeared to them.'

'And the angel told them the son of God had been born in Bethlehem,' said Frank, 'and they should go and see him.'

They sang some carols, and finally 'Jerusalem'. As they filed out, Harry Hardie shook the children by the hand and wished them a happy Christmas. Back in the playground they had a few minutes before lessons began again.

'That hymn, 'Jerusalem',' said Frank to the other boys, 'you know what it's saying, don't you?'

They looked at one another, uncertain what Frank was getting at.

'That Jesus came here, to England.'

'No he didn't,' said Alan.

'He did. With Joseph of Arimathea.'

At this Billy's ears pricked up. 'You mean the one who planted the hawthorn stick at Glastonbury?' he said.

'Yeah.'

'But he didn't come until after Jesus died. He had Jesus's blood in the Holy Grail.'

'He came before too, that's what my dad says. He reckons Joseph was a tin trader, and came to Cornwall with Jesus. Then they came up around here.'

This struck Billy as the most extraordinary thing, and that it should come from Frank made it all the more so.

'When Jesus was young?'

'Probably. Before he went into the wilderness, anyway.'

Miss Shute called them to their lessons, and they dashed back into the classroom. 'You don't know everything about Glaston-bury,' said Frank as they were sitting down.

'I never said I did,' said Billy. 'Maybe you can tell me more some time.'

★   ★   ★

Margaret had bought Leonora Vale a geranium, and she and Billy and Sarah walked to Tanyard Cottage to give it to her. Leonora was wearing a green plaid skirt and a red jumper, as though in anticipation of this Christmas call.

'You don't seem to have very much in the way of plants,' said Margaret. 'I thought this might brighten things up.'

'Oh, my plants are in the garden,' said Leonora. 'Not that there's much to see at the moment.'

All Billy had seen of Leonora's garden was a tangled patch at the front.

'Perhaps we could see it anyway?' said his mother.

Leonora led them through the room where the cats lived, and out of the back door. They stepped into a walled garden that Billy had never imagined could possibly be there. Though it was in its winter drab, this was a beautifully tended place. There were small apple and greengage trees trained against the walls, gnarled espaliers with lichen-covered branches, and row upon row of what in a few months would be a wonderful assortment of vegetables. At the end were a greenhouse and a rickety shed.

'It's a secret garden,' said Billy.

'Yes,' said Leonora, 'that's exactly what it is. And now you too know the secret.'

They walked slowly down the path between the vegetable patch and the flower border.

'Potatoes, beans, onions, carrots, cabbages,

parsnips,' said Leonora in a kind of litany. 'And over here there will be larkspur, helichrysum, tulips and roses.' They went inside the greenhouse and stood on the chilly stone floor, gazing up at the glass roof. 'Those are peach and nectarine,' said Leonora, pointing to spindly branches that clung to the wooden struts. There were a couple of cracked panes, but this entire space seemed to be cared for in a way that the house simply wasn't. They walked across to the shed, and Billy peeked in at the jumble of tools and pots and cans. He picked up one half of a broken pair of shears.

'What's this?' he asked.

'Oh, they're my non-secateurs,' said Leonora, smiling.

'But there's only one of them,' said Billy.

Leonora patted Billy on the head and said, 'Now you've ruined my little joke.'

'You are a sly one, Leonora,' said Margaret. 'You've kept this all to yourself.'

'As it should be. You know what Voltaire said, don't you?'

'No.'

'Well, he said simply that we must cultivate our garden. But what he was really saying was that the world's troubles would be greatly eased if we did.'

'I wish I had a garden like this,' said

Margaret. 'I did once, I suppose, but I had other people to look after it.'

'Then it wasn't really yours.'

They went back into the house, and Leonora put the kettle on.

'What are you doing on Christmas Day?' said Margaret.

'What I do every day, poppet. Why?'

'Would you like to come to our house for dinner?'

★ ★ ★

The first rehearsal of *Private Lives* took place on a very cold evening. Margaret drove carefully on her way into Wells, her desire not to be late wrestling with her fears about ice on the road. The others were all there by the time she arrived.

'We will do the first two scenes,' said Diana Mogg. 'Now, remember how important these are in establishing the characters and their relationships. All four of you are in an unsettled state. You are *giddy*.'

Margaret sat in the front row watching Bert Dampler and Liz Burridge rehearse the first scene. Liz projected more strongly than Margaret had thought she might. Bert on the other hand seemed too wet. He could manage a certain kind of flippancy, but there was something unconvincing about him in the end: she simply couldn't imagine him being rich. Which set her to wondering whether anyone would find *her* convincing as a rich woman. Well, she would just have to put it on. And the more her character was described by Elyot and Sybil Chase as being uncontrolled, wicked and unfaithful, the more determined she became to play it to the hilt.

'I don't believe I'm a bit like what you think I am,' she said as she took her turn on the stage.

'How do you mean?'

'I was never a poor child.'

'Figure of speech, that's all.'

'I suffered a good deal, and had my heart broken. But it wasn't an innocent, girlish heart. It was jagged with sophistication. I've always been sophisticated, far too knowing. That caused many of my rows with Elyot. I irritated him because he knew I could see through him.'

They came to the end of the scene. 'Good, Margaret,' said Diana. 'Now, Michael, you must be altogether more cynical. You don't really love Amanda, you've just persuaded yourself that you *should* love her. Let's try it again.'

They went back to the beginning, and this time Michael was better. He's feeling his way into it, thought Margaret, as we all are. As the evening wore on, she began to sense a determination in herself to make this as good as it could be. And she sensed something else, something she hadn't felt for a long time, which both exhilarated and appalled her: she began to feel the sharp promptings of ambition.

At the end of the rehearsal they all went to the Swan Hotel again. The euphoria of the audition evening was replaced now by a mood of realism, and an intimation that this apparently shallow play about selfish and foolish people would in fact be harder to bring off than they had supposed. Margaret made a point of sitting next to Liz.

'You're very good,' she said. 'You've got Sybil's . . . ' She broke off, trying to find the right word. The one she wanted to use was 'insecurity', but she didn't dare say it. In the end she said 'gaiety', which was not what she meant at all.

'You're very good too,' said Liz. 'You must have had lots of experience.'

'Experience of acting?'

Liz looked away for a moment. 'I mean you really *are* sophisticated. The rest of us . . . ' At this point she leaned towards Margaret, and spoke softly. 'The rest of us are just country people. But you know what it's like to be well off, to have style.'

Margaret wondered what Liz had been told about her, and was certain it must have been exaggerated. She was beginning to think that Liz's remarks might betray some sort of resentment.

'I think style is one of those things you can't buy,' said Margaret. 'You either have it or you don't. And may I say that I think you have it yourself.'

The evening broke up, and Margaret drove home. Gliding along the Launcherley road she felt for a few moments weightless, and abstracted from her life. What would it be like, she wondered, to be free of all this, of her responsibilities to Jim and the children, to her life as she knew it? She let her imagination carry her away. She was an actress on the West End stage, and Michael Ford her leading man and her lover. In her suite in the Savoy Hotel, she sat reading her notices and savouring the triumph of the opening night. Such thoughts quickly shamed her, and she set them aside. But she was unable to deny them, or to suppress them entirely.

Later, as she sat with Jim in the parlour, she found herself returning to the script, unable to leave it aside. She laughed out loud at one point.

'What's that?' said Jim.

'Oh, it's just Coward's way with words, that's all. 'Certain women should be struck regularly, like gongs.' That shouldn't be funny at all, but it is.'

'You're enjoying it, then?'

'I'm enjoying it very much.'

Jim put down the newspaper. 'Bert Dampler came into the shop the other day. He doesn't look the part, somehow.'

'Oh, he'll do. But I'm bound to say that we women are better than the men.'

'Who's playing the other woman?'

'A girl called Liz Burridge. She's a waitress in Goody's café. She's very young, but she's definitely got something.'

'Liz Burridge?' said Jim.

'Yes, do you know her?'

'Well, I've bumped into her in Goody's.' He picked up his newspaper. 'I see Macmillan's in trouble again,' he said.

6

On Christmas morning Jim set off in the car with Billy and Sarah to collect Leonora Vale. In the confined space Billy smelled the faint scent of urine that seemed to follow her everywhere, and he was now certain that it came from her rather than the cats. She really was a very strange person, seeming at some times to be very wise and at others very silly. He couldn't remember anyone outside the family ever being invited to Christmas dinner before, and he wondered what it was about Miss Vale that his mother found so fascinating.

'Happy Christmas,' she said when they arrived, handing Margaret an exuberantly wrapped bottle of whisky.

'Leonora, you shouldn't,' said Margaret.

'Oh, I think she should,' said Jim, smiling easily and taking the bottle from Margaret's hand.

The turkey from Alton's farm took hours to cook, but this time Margaret was prepared.

'And what did Father Christmas give you, poppet?' said Leonora to Sarah as they sat down to eat.

'There's no such thing as Father Christmas,' said Sarah emphatically. 'I've known that for ages.'

'You've known it since last Christmas,' said Jim.

'I always knew.'

'No you didn't,' said Billy. 'You used to ask me how he could get down so many chimneys in one night.'

Jim proposed a toast, and they drank to what he called 'companionship'.

'How is the play coming along?' said Leonora to Margaret.

'We've only had one rehearsal. But it's fun. And harder than I thought it would be.'

'Ah, Noël was always a deceiver. He made everything look so easy, when it wasn't at all.'

'Noël?' said Jim. 'You knew Noël Coward?'

'When we were very young, yes. We spent a few weekends together at Hambleton Hall, with Mrs Astley Cooper. She was a friend of Noël's boyfriend, Philip Streatfield.'

'I thought Noël was a boy's name,' said Billy.

'It is,' said Leonora.

'But only girls have boyfriends.'

Leonora swept her hand through her hair and gave his mother a supplicating look.

'He was a friend who happened to be a

boy,' said Margaret.

'Yes,' said Leonora. 'We were all children really, no more than eighteen or so.'

'What was he like?' said Billy.

Leonora looked at Billy and Sarah as if considering how much she could say. 'He was so young, so impressionable. He would follow Mrs Cooper around with a notebook, jotting down her *bon mots*.'

'What's a bonmow?'

'It's something clever that people say. Like 'only mad dogs and Englishmen go out in the midday sun'.'

'That's not clever at all,' said Sarah. 'Cats go out in the midday sun too. Lucy does.'

'How is Lucy?'

'She's got fleas,' she said, jamming her knife into a roast potato and sending it flying off her plate.

'So did you get to know Coward well?' said Margaret, rescuing the potato and cutting it up.

'Not well. I spent perhaps three or four weekends with him. And of course there was always such a houseful. One saw other people at meals and drinks, and played games in the evenings. But the men were usually off hunting during the day.'

'Not Coward, surely?'

'Well, let's just say he wasn't quite as

fastidious about hunting as Oscar Wilde.'

'Are you going to tell us you knew Oscar Wilde too?' said Jim.

Leonora laid her hand on his. 'Now, now, young man,' she said. 'I'm not *that* old.'

After dinner Billy and Sarah listened to Wilfred Pickles on the radio, visiting a children's hospital. Jim poured shots of whisky for himself and Margaret and Leonora, and later he drove Leonora home. When he returned he said to Margaret, 'She's a queer fish, your Miss Vale, but she's all right, I think.'

'She smells like a fish,' said Sarah.

'She smells like pee,' said Billy.

Margaret's eyes flashed suddenly. 'If I hear one more word like that from either of you, you'll spend the rest of Christmas in your room.'

Billy stared at his mother, astonished by the vehemence of her words.

'I'm sorry,' she said, beginning to stack the dishes. 'I think Leonora's a treasure, that's all.'

★　★　★

As Jim sat quietly in the Crown, he heard a voice from behind him say, 'I've been looking for you everywhere.'

'You only had to come to the shop,' said Jim.

'You and I need to have a word,' said Towker. 'Let's take a walk.'

They went out into Market Place, and began walking towards the gates of the palace. Towker was in an agitated state, and he pressed ahead of Jim and into the grounds.

'You've heard I've been arrested,' he said when they were alone. 'Receiving stolen goods.'

'What's that got to do with me?' said Jim.

'Come off it, Palmer,' said Towker harshly. He flicked away his cigarette butt. 'Smith grassed on me.'

Jim thrust his hands into his coat pockets. 'I was doing a favour for a friend,' he said. 'I was going to London anyway, and you asked me to drop off a few packages.'

'Very decent, I'm sure.'

Jim felt a shiver of fear run through him.

Towker glanced edgily around. 'Look,' he said at last, 'there's no reason why you need come into this. Smith couldn't care less. But I'm going to need a favour.'

Jim let out a slow breath and watched it mist in the still air. 'What sort of favour?' he said.

'Friend of mine needs a job.'

'I'm not an employment agency.'

'Just for a few weeks. He wants to get into the fashion business in London, and he needs someone to show him the ropes.'

Jim looked down at his feet. So, he thought, it's come to this. 'I'm supposed to give him the benefit of my vast experience, then, am I?' he said.

'It's simple,' said Towker. 'He spends a few weeks helping you out, you show him how the place works, and then you write a nice reference on Underhill's notepaper.'

'I don't need any help.'

Towker looked at him levelly. 'I think you do,' he said.

★　★　★

The cathedral loomed palely in the moonlight. Jim and Liz sat a little apart on the bench, not touching or even looking at one another. The cold evening air, which might have drawn them together, somehow caused them to huddle in their own spaces.

'Why didn't you tell me you were in the play?' he said.

'Why should I? There's lots of things I do that you don't know about.'

'But after Margaret's audition?'

'We haven't seen each other since then, remember?'

'It's Christmas. There's a lot going on.'

Liz turned and looked at him very directly. 'Jim, you're a nice man and all that, but I'm not sure this was a good idea.'

'Maybe we shouldn't see each other again.'

She sat in silence for a few moments. 'Is that what you want?' she said at last.

He gazed towards the cathedral. What did he want, really? He wished he knew.

'No, Liz, it isn't,' he said.

She shifted along the bench and rested her head on his shoulder. 'It isn't what I want either,' she said. 'But I'm in a play with your wife.'

He looked down at her, and Margaret's description flashed through his mind: 'She's very young, but she's definitely got something.' His thoughts drifted to Margaret. Here he was again, neglecting his wife and his children, chasing after someone who would soon enough pass out of his life. Was this what he wanted, really?

She took his hand and entwined his fingers in hers. 'Do you have the keys to the shop?' she said.

★   ★   ★

The new term began, and the children shivered in the barely heated classroom, the boys at the back etching patterns into the ice on the inside of the windows. A new sense of purpose had been instilled in those who would be taking the eleven-plus. Miss Shute was firmer now, less willing to indulge their whims, and to Billy the classroom was a place of work in a way it had never been before. In the playground the boys tore around for a few minutes to get warm, and then congregated in the far corner.

'I've been thinking about what you said before Christmas,' said Billy to Frank. 'About how Jesus came around here. I think you're right. It makes sense, doesn't it?'

'I expect so,' said Frank a little warily.

'Just think of all the things that have happened at Glastonbury. It was because Jesus went there and made it a holy place.'

'I didn't say he went to Glastonbury. Just around here somewhere.'

'But he must have come to Glastonbury. That's where Joseph of Arimathea came.'

Frank rested his long back against the wall and eyed Billy thoughtfully. 'My dad would know,' he said. 'You could talk to him about it.'

'Could I?'

'Don't see why not. Come back with me after school and we'll ask him.'

As Billy and Frank and Ed walked along

the Arminster road a bank of dark clouds massed above them. The boys looked up expectantly.

'It's going to snow,' said Frank.

'Oh, great!' said Billy. 'I want to see what it looks like in the country.'

The Willmott farm was a ramshackle place. The mud in the yard was covered with a rime of frost that the afternoon sun had left untouched. Paint peeled from the doors and windows, and there was a closed-in feeling to it. Billy felt apprehensive about entering this house full of giants. They went into the kitchen, and Frank's mother looked up from the stove.

'This is Billy Palmer,' said Frank. 'He wants to talk to Dad about Jesus.'

Mrs Willmott gazed fixedly at Billy. Like her husband and sons she was tall and rangy. 'Any boy who wants to know about Our Lord is welcome in this household,' she said.

Billy sat at the kitchen table while Frank went in search of his father. It was very like the kitchen at home, plain and dark; but there was a sadness about it, and about the whole house, that Billy sensed strongly and couldn't shake off.

Matthew Willmott stooped as he entered the kitchen. He was surely the largest man Billy had ever seen, his shirt-cuffs hanging open around his forearms and his trousers barely stretching to his ankles. He had the same reddish skin as Hubert Fosse, and his carrot-coloured hair shot up into the air above his forehead. Billy watched closely as he sat down on a wooden chair that disappeared under him.

'So, young man,' he said. 'you want to know about Jesus in Somerset, do you?'

'Yes, sir,' said Billy.

'You're a believer, then.'

'A believer?'

'You believe in God and Our Lord Jesus Christ.'

'Of course I do.'

Willmott shifted his weight and reached out for the teapot. 'Don't see you in church, though, do we?' he said.

'My dad and mum don't go very much.'

'Are they believers?'

'I think so.'

Willmott poured tea into a large mug and took a noisy draught from it. He looked at him in the sceptical way that Billy had come to know so well from Frank. 'Families should go to church together,' he said. 'Now, what can I tell you?'

'Frank said that when we sing 'Jerusalem' we're singing about Jesus coming to England.'

'That's right,' said Willmott, burying his

face again in the mug.

'Well, I know about Joseph of Arimathea, and I know all about King Arthur and everyone . . . '

'Those Arthurian stories are nonsense,' said Willmott, cutting Billy off. 'The only stories that are true are the ones in the Good Book.'

'You mean you don't think there was a King Arthur?'

'I think there were some heathen louts who latched on to the story of the Holy Grail, that's what I think.'

Billy wasn't sure what to make of this, but he knew that if he wanted to learn about Jesus in Somerset he'd better not contradict this frightening man. 'Will you tell me about Joseph and Jesus coming to England?' he asked quietly.

Willmott wiped his mouth with the back of his hand and sat back in the creaking chair.

'They came to St Just, in Cornwall, first,' he said. 'Joseph was Mary's uncle. Jesus disappears from the Gospels between the age of twelve and thirty. There must have been many things he did. One of them was to come to England with Joseph.'

'Joseph was a tin trader?'

'Yes. He was a Pharisee, a rich merchant.

Cornwall was the best place in the world then for tin. And when they were done in Cornwall, they sailed up the coast to the River Axe, and came to Priddy.'

'Where's Priddy?'

'Just north of Wookey Hole, where the caves are.'

'And what did they do there?'

'Traded for lead. There's lead everywhere around here.'

'Did they leave any sign that they'd been there?'

'Our Lord didn't need to leave any sign. His very existence was a sign.'

'So how do you know?'

Willmott looked sternly at Billy. 'I just know, that's all,' he said. He put his mug down firmly on the table, the noise ringing around the room, and then nodded wordlessly at his wife, who refilled it from the teapot.

Billy considered for a moment. 'And then they came to Glastonbury,' he said.

'No, Jesus never came to Glastonbury. Joseph came back after Jesus died.'

'Well I think Jesus must have come to Glastonbury. It's such a holy place.'

'Fine words, young man, but he didn't.'

Billy looked around the room, at the cobwebs in the corners of the ceiling and the ashes on the floor, and a thought occurred to him.

'You know when in the Bible the devil takes Jesus to the top of a hill, don't you?'

'"The devil taketh him up into an exceeding high mountain, and sheweth him all the kingdoms of the world, and the glory of them'',' said Willmott.

'Well I bet that mountain was Glastonbury Tor.'

Willmott harrumphed loudly. 'That was in Galilee,' he said.

'But how do you know?'

Willmott leaned towards Billy. 'I know because it says so in the Good Book.' He reached out his arm and Billy flinched, but Willmott only rested a hand on his. 'You may be mistaken about a few things, young Palmer, but I like your sincerity. There isn't enough of that around.'

The first flakes of snow had begun to fall. Frank looked towards the window and said to Billy and Ed, 'Let's go outside. Race you.'

They dashed out into the yard, where they stood with their arms outstretched and their mouths open, gathering as many flakes as they could. Suddenly there was a flash of lightning, and a few seconds later a roll of thunder. Billy had never known thunder and lightning with snow before. What had started as a flurry soon became a blizzard, obscuring the house and the barns and making the boys' figures indistinct. Frank whooped with joy. 'It's a sign, Billy,' he said. 'I think you're right about Jesus and Glastonbury. I think he's sending us a sign.' He scooped up a handful of snow and packed it tightly. 'And here's another sign,' he said, and threw the snowball at Billy, hitting him square on the chest. Billy threw one back at Frank, which exploded on the top of his head.

'Signs and wonders!' Frank shouted exultantly. 'Signs and wonders.'

★　★　★

Billy sheltered at the Willmott farm until the storm abated, and then began to trudge home. It was dark and the sky was rapidly clearing, bright stars taking the place of snowflakes above his head. The snow was deep on the ground by now, and for the last half-mile he felt as though he were wading. But none of this mattered to Billy. He was in an exalted state. The knowledge that Jesus had come to Glastonbury, and that he, Billy Palmer, had been the first to understand this, was thrilling. It put all his troubles in an entirely different perspective, his being at odds with Frank Willmott, his fearing that his father was a liar. What did any of that matter when he had solved the great mystery of Jesus's life?

The farm and the cottage eventually came into sight. The moment he stepped into the kitchen, everyone looked up.

'Where on earth have you been?' said Margaret.

'At the Willmott farm,' said Billy. 'Sarah was supposed to tell you. I was all right.'

'You said you were going to look for Jesus,' said Sarah.

Billy turned to Jim. 'Jesus came to Glastonbury Tor, Dad,' he said. 'I know it.'

'Is that what Matthew Willmott's been telling you?'

'No, I said it. And it's true.'

His father shook his head, but said nothing.

In bed that night Billy imagined Jesus and Joseph on the tor. It was a long time before he fell asleep. And when he awoke in the morning it was to a scene that was utterly transformed, dazzling in the bright sunshine.

'There'll be no school for you two this morning,' said Margaret as she shovelled snow away from the doorway.

'And no work for me,' said Jim. 'I'm going to have to phone Winnie, though.' He gazed out of the window.

'Can I come too?' said Billy.

Jim looked back at him. 'If you like,' he said.

'I'll get my wellingtons.'

Out in the yard, Billy struggled in the deep snow.

'Are you sure you want to do this?' said Jim.

'Of course. It's fun.'

There were just two colours in the world, blue and white. The snow lay in drifts in the fields, piled up against walls and hedges, and in the places where cows and sheep usually grazed there was a smooth emptiness. Billy ran his hand along gateposts and branches, brushing off their delicate fronds. The landscape below them was a great white sheet, the tor a pillow someone had left under it.

'It's so quiet, Dad,' he said.

'That's what happens when it snows. Remember 'Silent Night'?'

'Silent Day, that's what this is.'

It took them a long time to get to the village, and then Jim had to dig his way into the telephone box. Billy wanted to stay out as long as possible, and persuaded his father to sit with him on the wall of the bridge over the stream. There was a frill of ice at the edge of the water.

'Do you think the river might freeze over?' said Billy.

'No, it runs too fast.'

'That's a shame. We could have gone ice skating, like we used to in Bath.'

'You'll go ice skating again one day.'

Billy looked down at the grey water. 'Are we going to live here for ever now, until I grow up?' he said.

'For ever is a little longer than when you grow up, Billy.'

'But you know what I mean.'

'Yes, I know what you mean. Well, I'm not sure. We'll have to see how this job goes.'

'Is it a good job?'

Jim shrugged his shoulders and pulled out a packet of cigarettes. 'It's all right,' he said. 'It's better than no job at all.'

'Not as good as the Jaguar job, though.'

'No, not anything like as good as that.'

Billy looked behind him at the school, which stood as quiet as on a Sunday, and then back at his father. The thought of his Dinky toys returned, as it had so often lately. His father might not be able to sell real Jaguars any more, but that hadn't stopped him from selling toy ones. He felt an urge to challenge his father's explanations for things, his easy turning aside of the questions Billy wanted answers to.

'Dad,' he said, 'why did you have to close the garage? Mum said you made some mistakes.'

His father lit a cigarette. He inhaled deeply and said, 'Did she now? Well, she was probably right.'

'What happened, then?'

Jim looked at the cigarette in his cold hand. 'If you want to know the truth, I was a bloody fool. I wanted too much.'

'Too much what?'

'Oh, too much money, too many things, too many envious looks from other people. The usual.'

'So that's why you had to close the garage?'

'I had to close the garage because I wanted to sell something that not enough people wanted to buy. If I'd stuck with Austins I'd have been fine. But then you and I wouldn't have been able to ride around in that Mark Eight, would we?'

'I'm glad we've got a car again now, even if it's only a Standard.'

'So am I.' Jim paused for a moment. 'I suppose we have a few things to be glad about, don't we?' he said. 'But it's still not enough.'

Billy studied his father closely as he gazed into the distance.

'I want to leave my mark,' Jim continued. 'I

don't want to have to ask myself one day what it was all about.'

'I'm going to leave my mark,' said Billy. 'I'm going to be a famous explorer.'

Jim flicked cigarette ash into the water. 'I'm sure you are,' he said.

★   ★   ★

When the bell rang early in the morning, Jim's heart sank. He knew very well who this must be.

He was a thin, languid young man. The features of his face were finely drawn, but his upper lip seemed to have trouble closing over his lower. He was smoking a cigarette, and held his hand away from his body in a gesture that Jim suspected he had learned from some film.

'I'm Tony Lewis,' he said. 'Nuncle sent me.'

'Nuncle?'

'Gordon Towker. Mr Towker to you.'

He was probably about seventeen or eighteen. Along with his attempt at an air of sophistication came a contemptuous gaze. He looked around the shop.

'So this is where I'm going to learn about the fashion business, is it?' he said.

'No,' said Jim. 'This is where you're going to learn about selling clothes.'

'An important distinction.'

'Yes. And let's get one or two other things straight while we're at it. I'm doing you a favour, and I expect you to be suitably grateful. There won't be much for you to do, but I want it done properly. Understood?'

'Of course, Jimmy. You don't mind if I call you Jimmy, do you?'

'I do, actually.'

Lewis looked at him calculatingly. 'Still I think I'll call you Jimmy,' he said. '*Actually*.'

Jim had come across men like Lewis in the war, but none as nancy as this. He was in for a difficult few weeks, he was quite sure.

'I'm going to show you the stock sheet and where everything is,' he said, trying to suppress his rising anger. 'Which is more than Reg Underhill did for me, I can tell you.'

He spent the morning showing Tony Lewis around. The boy showed no sign of having registered anything Jim told him. After a while he sat down on the stool and put his feet up on the counter. He leaned back his head and blew a perfect smoke ring into the air. Jim hadn't seen anyone do that for years.

'I'm going to London, you know,' said Lewis.

'So I hear.'

'I'm going to work for Hardy Amies.'

'You are?'

'Well, he doesn't know it yet. But he will.' He blew another smoke ring. 'Then, when I've conquered the London scene, I'll go to Paris and work for Pierre Cardin.'

'You seem to have it all worked out.'

'Yes I have, *actually*.'

'So what are you waiting for?'

'You know very well what I'm waiting for. A year's experience in the trade.'

'A year?' said Jim plaintively.

'Well, that's what it'll say on the reference you're going to write me.'

'I'll write anything you want me to now, today.'

'Not so hasty, Jimmy. There are things I can learn here. But don't worry, I won't be in your nest for very long.'

Jim had no intention of leaving Lewis in the shop at lunchtime, and he emptied the till and prepared to lock up as usual for an hour. As he was about to put the takings in the safe, Lewis said, 'I'll need some money.'

'That wasn't part of the deal,' said Jim.

'I don't mean wages. Pocket money.' He reached out a long arm and whisked away two pound notes. 'That'll do,' he said. 'Fivers are so difficult to change, don't you find?'

Jim thought for a moment about trying to take them back, but decided against it.

'So what's with you and Gordon Towker, then?' he said.

'Me and Nuncle?' said Lewis. 'Oh, we're just friends.'

'Nothing more than that?'

A look of distaste came over Lewis's features. 'Gordon Towker?' he said. 'I wouldn't touch him with a bargepole.' Then he looked directly at Jim. 'But a man like you, well that would be a very different matter.'

★   ★   ★

Jim and Margaret drove to the New Year's Eve party at the Moggs' house in Wells quite late in the evening. They had once again relied on Hubert Fosse to take care of the children, and didn't want him to have to stay too long.

'He seemed a bit fed up about it this time,' said Margaret.

'He shouldn't be,' said Jim. 'I gave him the whisky bottle as we were leaving.'

'I wonder how many people we'll know.'

'You'll know one person and I'll know no one.'

'I hope you're going to enter into the spirit of it.'

'I'll be the life and soul of the party,' said Jim with a wry smile.

The Moggs lived in a large house off the Cheddar road. When they arrived, Diana greeted them boisterously.

'Ah, Amanda Prynne and her current consort,' she said; and to Jim, 'how very good to meet you.'

Peter Mogg was a doctor at Melborne House, and most of the guests were either doctors or teachers. Michael Ford was the only other member of the *Private Lives* cast, and along with him, Jim and Margaret were the youngest people there. An elderly man introduced himself as Robert Erwin, the headmaster of the Boys' Blue School.

'Our boy should be joining you next year,' said Jim.

'It's highly competitive these days,' said Erwin. 'I'm afraid it's not enough just to pass the eleven-plus. He'll have to come to the school for interview.'

Margaret was approached by Michael, and Jim watched her out of the corner of his eye. He hadn't seen his wife like this for a long time now, and he was struck by how much at ease she seemed. She's spent the past months holed up in a tiny cottage, he thought, with only me, the children and Hubert Fosse for company. No wonder she's reached out to Leonora Vale and the theatrical society.

A man came up to Erwin, and in turn was

introduced to Jim as Jack Oakley, the owner of the Regal.

'I met your Bert Dampler the other day,' said Jim. 'He's in a play with my wife.'

'Yes, of course.' He leaned towards Jim and said, 'I fancy that young man's future lies *behind* the stage rather than on it.'

He was in his sixties, slightly stooped, with sharp, inquisitive green eyes and terrible teeth. His smile was faintly mischievous, but he closed it down quickly, as though to conceal the ruin of his mouth.

'Are you a cinema-goer?' he said.

'Well, I used to be, but it's difficult now, living in the country.'

'People are watching more and more television these days,' said Oakley. 'It's getting harder to compete.'

'You should show the sort of films you can't see on television, like Hitchcock's.'

'I'm afraid they might go over the heads of some of my customers,' said Oakley. 'Ealing comedies are what go down well here, them and war films.'

Before long Diana Mogg clapped her hands and announced that it was one minute to twelve. She turned on the radio, and as Big Ben started to chime, Jim and Margaret joined the others in counting down to midnight.

'Happy New Year,' said Jim, and he kissed Margaret and held her to him. 'Happy nineteen fifty-nine.'

She rested her head against his shoulder. 'It'll be a better year,' she said, 'won't it?'

'I can't see how it can be any worse.'

They were home by half past twelve. Hubert sat rather still in the most comfortable chair, and Jim could tell at a glance that the level of the whisky bottle had dropped precipitously. He walked him across the yard and made sure he was safe inside his rooms. When he went upstairs, Margaret was standing by the bed in her slip.

The dim light accentuated the lines of her body. He eased the straps over her shoulders, and the slip fell to the floor. Margaret wrapped her arms around his neck.

'Get under the blankets, sweetheart,' he said.

She pressed herself to him. 'No,' she said. 'I want to see you.'

★　★　★

'When we were together, did you really think I was unfaithful to you?' said Amanda Prynne.

'Yes, practically every day,' said Elyot Chase.

'I thought you were too; often I used to torture myself with visions of your bouncing around on divans with awful widows.'

'Why widows?'

'I was thinking of Claire Lavenham really.'

'Oh, Claire.'

'What did you say 'Oh, Claire' like that for? It sounded far too careless to me.'

'What a lovely creature she was.'

Diana Mogg sprang up from her seat, crying, 'Bert, you must be *wistful* when you say that. The whole point of this scene is to maintain the tension between Elyot and Amanda, the feeling that they are still in love but still distrust one another too. *Wistful* now, Bert. Try it again.'

They were only a few weeks away from the first night, and a sense of urgency was beginning to creep in. Margaret found herself more and more exasperated by Bert and Michael's failure to understand the essence of the play. For her part, Margaret had immersed herself in it to a degree she found a little disconcerting. She so much wanted it to be a success now. She and Diana had tacitly joined forces, and Margaret had become in effect the deputy director. She urged the others on, prompted them when they stumbled over their lines, and made her own suggestions about tone and emphasis. Into the dark and empty space of the theatre she ushered visions of the balcony at Deauville and the apartment in Paris that were almost startling in their clarity. And then she had to remind herself that she had never even been abroad.

The cast dispersed at the end of the rehearsal, and Margaret and Liz found themselves the only ones inclined to go to the Swan for a drink.

'The men aren't strong enough,' said Margaret as they sat down by the fireplace.

'When are they ever?' said Liz.

'Maybe Coward meant the women to be more interesting than the men. But when we come to a line such as 'Elyot and me, we were like two violent acids bubbling about in a nasty matrimonial bottle', I'm reminded that Bert Dampler hasn't got a clue what a matrimonial bottle might be like.'

Liz smiled. 'None of the rest of us have,' she said. 'Remember you're the only married person in the cast.'

'Yes, of course,' said Margaret, sighing. 'I'm being too hard on them. And it's not as though we're much better.' She looked across at Liz, at the supple figure sitting rather too straight in the leather armchair. 'What about you, Liz? Do you have a boyfriend?'

Liz looked into the fire and then abruptly back at Margaret. 'Nobody special,' she said. 'Why do you ask?'

Margaret shrugged. 'I'm sorry, I'm just curious. You're such an attractive girl. I'm surprised Michael or Bert haven't been hanging around you.'

'Michael did make a pass once, but I don't care for him. He thinks he's a charmer. I don't like that.'

'What *do* you like in men?'

Liz shifted uneasily in her chair. She was avoiding Margaret's gaze now.

'I like a man to be attentive, but not smarmy,' she said at last.

'Don't we all.'

They sat silent then, Liz apparently mesmerized by the flames of the fire. Margaret realized that she barely knew her.

'What are your plans, Liz?' she said. 'What are you going to do with your life?'

'I'm going to nursing school in Bristol after Easter.'

'I couldn't imagine you staying at Goody's for very long.'

'That's just a way of filling in time. They weren't able to take me last September.'

'Do you know Bristol?'

'I've been there once, for the interview.'

'It'll be very different from here.'

Liz looked up at Margaret again. 'I want it to be as different as possible,' she said.

★   ★   ★

When the very cold weather was over, trade became brisker in the shop. Jim had mastered the essentials, and was quietly satisfied that there appeared to have been no falling off in takings since Reg's stroke. All he needed now was to see the back of Tony Lewis, and then he could begin to prepare for the spring and summer consignments.

One morning Norman Elsworth from Herrings came in looking for a new jacket.

'When are you going to wear it?' said Jim.

'Every day,' said Elsworth.

'To tweed or not to tweed, then, that is the question,' said Lewis.

Elsworth gave him a sour look. 'I can make up my own mind, thank you,' he said.

Jim took out a couple of jackets, one in plain grey and the other in a Prince of Wales check. 'Too fancy,' said Elsworth of the second, and he tried on the grey one. It was a little tight in the shoulders, and after a few moments' straightening, Jim suggested he try a larger size.

'Very dapper, I'm sure,' said Lewis. He stood behind the counter with his arms akimbo, turning his head this way and that.

'It's perfect,' said Jim. 'And it'll serve for any occasion.'

'Jackets are longer this season,' said Lewis, 'with softer shoulder padding and slim-cut lapels.'

'They may be in Savile Row,' said Jim, 'but in Market Place in Wells this is how they are.'

Elsworth paid for his jacket and left. As soon as he was out of the door, Jim turned on Lewis.

'I can put up with your doing sweet fuck-all around here,' he said, 'but I won't tolerate that kind of talk with customers, understand?'

'I don't think Nuncle would like to hear you speaking to me in that way.'

'Well Nuncle isn't here, is he?'

'Not at this very moment, no.'

Lewis stared impassively at Jim. What do people think is going on in here? Jim wondered. It must be obvious that there was something odd about this arrangement, especially since he continued to close the place at lunchtime. He went into the office and began drawing up an order to send to Askews. Out in the shop he could hear Lewis chuckling for no one's benefit but his own.

★ ★ ★

Billy sat across the desk from the headmaster, his father and mother on either side of him. Robert Erwin seemed fantastically old, his wrinkly face and wild white hair making him look like a ghost.

'So, Billy,' he said, 'you want to come to the Blue School.'

'Yes, sir.'

'First you have to pass your eleven-plus, as you know.'

'I'm taking it soon.'

'We are able to offer places on the understanding that they may be claimed if you pass. But we need to know a little about boys before we can do that.'

Billy looked expectantly at the headmaster, who was reading from a sheaf of papers, and then cast his eyes around the room. In a corner stood a huge globe, the biggest he'd ever seen, and he had to resist the impulse to get up and give it a spin. He looked back across the leather-topped desk at the man who held his fate in his hands.

'Your teacher gives you high praise, young man,' he said. 'You're particularly interested in literature and history.'

'Yes, sir.'

He laid down the papers and took off his glasses. 'What are you reading now?' he said.

'*Kidnapped*, sir.'

'Ah, David Balfour. Boys like David Balfour, don't they?'

'Well, he's a boy like us.'

'He's scarcely a boy, as I recall. He must be sixteen or so.'

'But he's not a grown-up.'

Erwin looked at him thoughtfully for a few moments.

'So what do you think of Bonnie Prince Charlie?' he said.

'I haven't got that far.'

'Oh, he's not in it. But surely Alan Breck talks about him?'

'Was he the one who tried to get Scotland back from the English?'

'Precisely.'

'Then I think he's all right, sir. I think Scotland should have its own king.'

Erwin nodded as if to express agreement. 'Do you now?' he said. 'And what about Wales?'

'Wales too. Some people think King Arthur was from Wales.'

'But you don't?'

'No, sir. He was from here.'

He picked up the papers again and put on his glasses. After a few moments he said, 'So what do you want to be when you grow up?'

Before Billy could answer, his father said,

'His head's full of ideas, Mr Erwin, like all boys'.'

'I want to be an explorer,' said Billy, a note of defiance entering his voice. His head wasn't full of ideas at all; it just had one.

'What kind of explorer?'

'I don't know. Just someone who explores new places.'

'And where would you like to explore?'

Billy considered this question carefully, gazing once again at the globe.

'I think there are bits of China that haven't been explored,' he said at last.

'Not even by the Chinese?'

'I don't mean by the Chinese. I mean by us, the English.'

'So a place hasn't been explored until the English have been there?'

'Not properly, sir. After all, we invented exploration, didn't we?'

Erwin smiled weakly, and Jim shifted in his seat.

'There have been a few Scots explorers too, you know,' said Erwin.

'Oh, they count too.'

He looked benignly at Billy. 'You seem well disposed towards the Scots,' he said. 'You must have guessed that I'm one myself.'

'No, sir, I didn't.'

'All the better then.'

On the way home they stopped at the village shop, and Margaret bought groceries while Jim and Billy sat in the car. A young woman passed by pushing a pram, and Jim wound down the window.

'Good morning, Mrs Burnham,' he said. 'How's the baby?'

'Teething,' said the woman wearily. 'There's not a wink of sleep to be had.'

As she walked on, it dawned on Billy that now was the time. He had intended to ask his mother, but today he felt bold enough to talk to his father. 'Dad,' he said. 'Will you tell me about babies, one day?'

Jim twisted in his seat to face Billy. 'If you want,' he said, and then, 'I suppose I should have done before now, shouldn't I?'

Jim suggested that Margaret drive home alone, so that he and Billy could take a walk. As they crossed the footbridge, Jim said, 'So you're getting hard sometimes, I expect.'

'Yes,' said Billy.

'You're dreaming about girls.'

'No, not really. I'm dreaming about mountains.'

'Girls and mountains have a lot in common.'

'Do they?'

Jim smiled and said, 'No, not really.'

They began to ascend the slope towards

home, and then Jim said, 'So you know what you do with it?'

'Some boys have told me, but it seems strange.'

'It does at first,' said Jim. 'Then soon it doesn't at all.'

'So what happens after you've put it inside a girl?'

'Well, she has an egg in her.'

'An egg? You mean like a chicken's egg?'

'Well, it doesn't have a shell. But it's an egg. And it's fertilized by the man's seed. Then it grows into a baby, and nine months later it's born.'

They stopped at a gate and looked across at the tor. 'It may sound odd,' said Jim, 'but it's actually very nice. It's so nice that people do it all the time, even when they aren't making babies. You don't just put your willy inside her, you kiss her and touch her all over.'

Billy sensed that a moment had arrived, an opportunity to talk to his father properly.

'If people do it when they're not making babies,' he said, 'do they do it even when they're not married?'

Jim looked away from him and shifted his weight uneasily. 'Sometimes,' he said.

'Have you done it with other people, with people who aren't Mum?'

'I'm not sure that's any of your concern.'

'But I want to know the facts of life,' said Billy insistently. 'That's what they're called, aren't they?'

His father remained silent for a long time. 'Well then, yes I have,' he said. 'But there's no reason your mother should know, understand?'

'Do you do it with Liz Burridge?'

The instant the words were out of his mouth he regretted them. His father turned on him angrily.

'Who said anything about Liz Burridge?' he demanded.

Billy looked away. 'I saw you,' he said.

'You saw me what?'

'I saw you in the car with her, when I went to the Regal. You said you were going to Bath.'

Jim let out a sound that was something between a sigh and a groan. He hung his head and said nothing.

'I'm sorry,' said Billy. 'I wasn't sneaking. We just went to look at the Blue School, and I saw the car.'

Jim looked at Billy for a few moments. 'I'm the one who should be sorry,' he said. 'I'm the one who should be bloody sorry.'

★ ★ ★

Jim told himself over and over that he shouldn't see Liz again, but something always drew him back. He took her to Shepton Mallet for dinner, reckoning that to be seen with her in Wells was too risky now. The King's Arms was a pretty inn set back from a quiet square away from the centre of the town. Through the leaded windows a soft yellow light beckoned them in. In the bar the wooden beams were hung with brass tankards and horseshoes. They sat drinking white wine and studying the ornate menu, Jim watching Liz closely as she ordered. She was ill at ease with this sort of formality, it was plain to see. They went through to the dining room and sat at a candle-lit table by the window.

'The woman must always sit facing into the room,' said Jim.

'Why's that?'

'So that she may be admired by the other diners.'

She smiled, and relaxed into her chair.

'I'm going to London next week,' she said, 'for the first time.'

'What are you going to do there?'

'My mother's taking me on a shopping trip. She's going to kit me out for Bristol.'

'I'd forgotten about Bristol. How long is it now?'

'Two months.'

'Selfridges,' said Jim. 'That's the place for good clothes at reasonable prices.'

'You sound like an advert,' she said, smiling mischievously.

'Do I? Maybe I'm spending too much time in that shop.'

'You're spending all your time in that shop. It's your job.'

'Don't remind me.'

Their prawn cocktail starters arrived. As she picked up her fork, Liz said, 'There's a man over there who keeps staring at us.'

'Men are always staring at us,' said Jim. 'They're jealous.'

'I don't think this one's got any reason to be jealous. The woman he's with is a stunner.'

They returned to talk of London, to the things Liz might cram into a single day there. Then she looked beyond him and whispered, 'He's coming over.'

'My dear Jim,' said the man. Jim turned in his chair to see the elegant figure of David Latymer.

'Hello, David.'

There was an awkward silence. 'This is Liz Burridge,' he said.

'How do you do, young lady,' said Latymer. His pale eyes scrutinized Liz closely.

'Liz is the daughter of a friend from Wells.'

'And you've decided to explore the delights of Shepton.'

'It's very nice,' said Liz.

'It's quiet. It doesn't have the tourist attractions of Wells. And that suits us very well.' With this he gestured towards the table he was sitting at, and Jim looked across to see Clare Latymer waving at him. He smiled tightly.

'Well, I should leave you to your tête-à-tête,' said Latymer. He bowed to Liz, nodded at Jim, and returned to his wife.

'Who was that?' said Liz as soon as he was out of earshot.

'David Latymer. He owns the Charlton Cider Company. They live in the big house near ours. That's when they're not in their mansion in London.'

'He's got rich written all over him.'

Their conversation became uneasy. Jim was drinking a lot, and he reminded himself that he would have to drive home in the dark. Eventually Liz said, 'They're leaving.'

'That's torn it,' he said after they'd gone.

'Will they tell your wife?'

'No. We never see them. It's just that . . . oh, I don't know: there seems nowhere we can go these days.'

She laid a hand on his, and stroked it with her thumb. 'We'll find places,' she said.

They returned to the lounge after dinner, and Jim ordered a whisky. The other diners had left, and though it was barely half past nine they had the place to themselves. Jim swirled the liquor in the heavy glass.

'Do you know what I think, Liz?' he said suddenly. 'I think I'm a failure.'

She looked at him with a startled expression. 'Just because you're not as rich as David Latymer?'

'No, that's not what I mean. I've messed up my life.'

'You've had some problems, that's all.'

He looked at her thoughtfully. 'I've had a barrow-load of problems, Liz. And whose fault is that?'

'But you said it was the times, the rationing and that.'

'Did I now?' he said wearily. He watched the light reflecting off the amber liquid in his glass. 'Well, I've always been good at finding other things or other people to blame.'

She looked away from him. 'And I suppose you think you're a failure as a husband too?' she said.

He gazed at her profile, at the soft mouth and the lovely line that described her throat and neck. 'Maybe,' he said. 'How do you measure that, though? Does the fact that I'm here with you rather than at home with my wife mean I've failed as a husband?'

She turned towards him. 'Only you can know that,' she said.

Jim weaved his way back to Wells, knowing he shouldn't be behind the wheel. Market Place was silent beneath the towers of the cathedral, and the key screeched in the door of the shop as he opened it. He left the lights off, and they felt their way towards the office. Closing the door behind them, he turned to Liz and took her in his arms. They made love in the clumsy sort of way he hated, and soon they were saying good night out in the street. He didn't offer to escort her home, but got straight in the car and drove out onto the Glastonbury road.

The whisky was doing strange things to his eyes. The familiar road seemed now to veer in unexpected directions, and to fork into two when he knew very well that it shouldn't. He slowed down, but still the road deceived him, causing him to turn too sharply or not sharply enough. Near Launcherley Farm a dog appeared from nowhere and ran in front of him. He jammed on the brakes, and having come to a halt he was suddenly afraid of going on.

He opened the door and got out, inhaling the frosty air deeply. Reaching back into the car he switched off the engine and the lights, and lit a match to a cigarette. He felt swathed in the dark silence, and consoled by it. Consoled for being a bankrupt, for being an adulterer, for being a lousy father. He stood there for a long time, leaning against the side of the car, his eyes fixed on the intermittent glow of the cigarette.

★ ★ ★

'We just weren't thinking,' said Margaret.

Dr Enright looked at her in a way that she took to be mildly reproving. How could she explain that it had been the first time in months?

'How old are you?'

'Thirty-six.'

'We'll need to do some tests, then. One must be careful later in life.'

So this was later in life, thought Margaret. How odd: she felt as though she were just beginning.

'Where would you like to have it?'

'Is there any choice?'

'There's Wells Infirmary or home. I wouldn't recommend home, of course; but some women prefer it.'

'The Infirmary,' said Margaret. 'I had Billy and Sarah in hospital.'

'Good. I will refer you to Dr Morton.'

She walked home very slowly. The snows had cleared, and winter's grip was loosening. She leaned against a gate and looked towards Glastonbury. What would the children think, she wondered, of the idea of another brother or sister? And what would Jim think? As she considered this she knew she wouldn't tell him, at least not for a while. Her hand went to the place. Jim had had his secrets, and she would have hers.

Billy and Sarah were already home by the time she returned.

'Where have you been, Mummy?' said Sarah.

'To the doctor's.'

'Are you ill?'

'I've got a funny tummy.'

'Let me rub it.'

Margaret sat down at the kitchen table while Sarah stroked her awkwardly. She put a hand up to Sarah's hair, and drew her to her breast. She will be thrilled, of course, she thought. And she will be a great help, especially when she's older. Margaret so much wanted to tell her now. But she must wait. And Jim must wait too.

★　★　★

Margaret sat in Leonora's sitting room reading the last pages of *Tess of the D'Urbervilles*. The fire had gone out, and the room felt cold and cheerless.

'I've seen many more tears on the faces of beautiful women than on plain ones,' said Leonora eventually.

'Is that fate?' said Margaret.

'Everything's fate, poppet.'

She went into the kitchen to make a cup of tea, and when she returned Margaret noticed that the sole of one of her shoes was flapping loosely.

'Your shoes are in a terrible state,' she said.

Leonora looked down abstractedly. 'Well, I hardly notice.'

'You need a new pair,' said Margaret firmly. 'Something warm and dry for these chilly days.'

'I don't recall the last time I bought a pair of shoes,' said Leonora. 'In fact I don't recall the last time I bought anything that wasn't from the village shop.'

'Then I think a shopping trip is called for. Let's go to Wells on Saturday.'

They drove into town on a damp, windswept morning. The streets were quiet for a Saturday, the shops empty. Leonora bought a pair of suede bootees with sheepskin linings, and then they went to Browne's nursery to buy seeds. 'I'll start them in the greenhouse,' she said, 'and then put them in the garden in the spring.'

Margaret noticed that very soon Leonora began to show signs of fatigue. 'Let's go to the tearooms for a coffee,' she said.

Leonora sat down gratefully at the table, and smoothed the gingham tablecloth. 'I'm quite worn out,' she said.

'You're not used to it,' said Margaret. 'You must get out more. I think we should make this a regular occurrence.'

Margaret ordered coffee, and a cake for Leonora. She looked around the room, at the other women sipping their tea. She was the youngest person there by twenty years, and she felt as though she were intruding on some sort of communion.

'The play must be getting close,' said Leonora.

'Yes,' she replied, and then she smiled ruefully. 'I think it's turning me into a shrew.'

'Why a shrew?'

'Oh, I don't know. I want it to be perfect, and of course it can't be. So I'm taking it out on the others.'

'Drama is exacting,' said Leonora. 'There's no point if it isn't, even in amateur productions.'

'That's what I think.'

'I saw it once, years ago. Not the original, though. That would have been something.'

'Who was in the original?'

'Larry Olivier was Victor, and your part was played by Gertrude Lawrence. Coward wrote the play with her in mind. And he played Elyot Chase himself.'

'It's very intricate. It must have taken him a long time.'

Leonora snorted. 'He wrote it in four days, in a hotel room in Shanghai. He was laid up with flu.'

'That's extraordinary.'

'Not really. The characters were all based on his cronies. Elyot and Amanda were the Castlerosses, a famously tempestuous couple.'

Margaret held her cup in both hands and gazed into it. 'He's so good on love, isn't he? He knows how frail it is.'

'Frail? That's an odd word to use.'

Margaret put down her cup and pushed it away from her. 'My husband's having an affair,' she said calmly. 'I've had my suspicions for a while, but now I think I know who it is.'

Leonora looked at her directly. 'I thought things were better between you,' she said.

'So did I. It's strange that it's only now that I can sense it. He might have had a dozen affairs in the autumn for all I knew. But in the past weeks he hasn't been able to hide it.'

'And who is she?'

Margaret looked down at the tablecloth. 'Ah, well that's rather awkward,' she said. 'If I'm right, that is. It's one of my fellow cast members, a girl called Liz Burridge.'

'And who is Liz Burridge?'

'She's a child, really. She can't be more than eighteen or nineteen. She works at Goody's café down the street, and she's going to be a nurse.'

'She sounds about right,' said Leonora tartly. She put her hand on Margaret's. 'I'm sorry, I shouldn't have said that.'

'You can say anything you wish. She's pretty and very impressionable. About right, just as you say.'

She dropped Leonora off on the way home. As she entered the kitchen she sensed a stillness in the place. Billy was reading in the children's room, Jim sat in the parlour, and Sarah was playing half-heartedly with her cookery set.

'Did you buy anything for me?' said Sarah.

'No I didn't. This was for Leonora, as you very well know.'

Sarah rested her chin in her hands and looked at her mother sulkily.

'What have you been making?' said Margaret.

'I can't make anything without you, can I? Daddy's no help at all.'

Margaret went into the parlour and gave Jim a kiss on the cheek. 'You're all very glum this morning', she said.

'Are we? That's because we haven't had you around.'

She brushed her hand through his thick hair. How does she see him? she wondered. Does Liz Burridge see an attentive man, or does she see what I see: a man who needs attention?

7

It was weeks now since they'd got the car, and throughout that time the matter of the tor, and of their going there, seemed to Billy to be something he dare not speak of. It was very clear to him that his father could afford the petrol if he wished. He was denying Billy the thing he most wanted. But why? His bafflement only increased when one day Jim suggested they all go to the caves at Wookey Hole. Billy told himself this must be some sort of step along the way, some sort of test perhaps. And anyway, he was excited by the prospect of this trip. His imagination was fired by the idea of a river flowing underground, of caves where people used to live. Impatient for it, he decided the day before that he would go up into the hills between the village and Wells to try and see where the caves were.

He was quite steady on his bike now, and went further than he had ever done before. The ride into the village was downhill practically all the way, and he felt like a bird swooping in on it, the cold air blowing his hair flat against the top of his head. A bridleway led off Dark Lane, and he dumped the bike in the bushes and set off. The sun was low and watery, and he wondered how far he would be able to see. Following a path that rose steeply through a wood, he came out on the edge of a stony field. A fox slunk out of the trees, doubling back the moment it saw him.

On the far side of the field was a beech covert. All Billy had to do was to get to the other side of it for the view of Wells to open up. The cathedral dominated everything. He tried to picture what it must have looked like hundreds of years ago, when the cathedral was first built. No wonder people went to churches like this: they were so much bigger and grander than anything else.

The Mendip Hills curled gently around the town. Wookey Hole was just beyond Wells, he'd been told, but where? The haze made things indistinct, and for now he would just have to imagine it. He was desperately disappointed. Why did he have to rely on his father to go to places like Glastonbury and the caves? He turned back into the covert and ran across the field, telling himself that at least now he had some idea of where he was going.

That night, like so many nights now, he lay awake for ages. Images of caves and rivers coursed through his mind. Unable to settle, he crept down the stairs to get a glass of milk. The stairs creaked, and as he climbed them again, a candle appeared in the doorway of his parents' room.

'Billy?' said his mother.

'I can't sleep,' he said. 'I'm too excited.'

She rested a hand on his shoulder. 'You don't want to be tired in the morning, do you?' she said. 'Go back to bed and count sheep.'

'That never works.'

'Count the stars, then.'

The next morning they set off early. Sarah was reluctant to go.

'There's three big caves,' said Billy, 'and one of them has a witch in it.'

'That's Miss Shute,' said Sarah. 'That's where she lives.'

'I do wish you'd stop talking about your teacher in that way,' said Jim. 'She is *not* a witch, do you understand?'

She folded her arms and stared out of the car window.

'And I don't want any pouting from you, young lady.'

'I'm not pouting, I'm feeling my teeth with my tongue.'

'No you're not,' said Billy, 'you're pouting. You always do when you're told off.'

'You stay out of this,' said Jim.

'Why? She's always spoiling things.'

'No I'm not,' said Sarah.

Jim pulled over and turned in his seat to face them. 'Look,' he said, 'if you two can't stop squabbling we'll just go home.'

Billy looked away from his father. Why was he so cross, he wondered, on this of all days? He glanced appealingly at Margaret, who gave him the tight-lipped expression she always used when arguments broke out.

They walked past the paper mill to the entrance of the caves, and stood looking out over the river as it gushed from the side of the cliff. 'They used to chase animals over these cliffs,' said Jim, 'and then come down here to get them.'

'Then what did they do?' said Sarah.

'Eat them, of course.'

'Yuck!'

'We eat animals, don't we?' said Billy. 'We'll probably eat bits of Stan and Gertie one day.'

'No we won't!' said Sarah. 'I'll never eat Gertie, ever.'

There were half a dozen other people on their tour, including three who spoke in strange accents and wore brightly coloured clothes.

'They're Americans,' said Jim. 'That's how they dress.'

Billy stared at the boy, who was a couple of years older than him. He wore a red jacket, blue trousers, and yellow socks. Billy had never seen yellow socks before, not even on a girl. He couldn't take his eyes off them.

The guide gathered them together and began his talk, and then they ducked into the strange gloom of the first chamber. Electric lights hung here and there, picking out the deep reds and browns and blacks of the rocks. There was water dripping from above, and the damp chilled Billy, even though it was warmer here than outside.

'I don't think I want to stay in here for very long,' said Sarah.

Margaret held her hand. 'You'll be fine,' she said. 'This is going to be exciting.'

In a larger, deeper chamber the river flowed gently by. The water was astonishingly clear, throwing off a ghostly green light. Billy slipped on the wet stone, and clutched at a rock to right himself.

'This is the Witch's Kitchen,' said the guide. He shone his torch at a huge stalagmite that grew out of the floor of the cave. 'And there she is, turned to stone when a monk sprinkled her with holy water.' The rock looked remarkably like a witch's head, with a bonnet, a hooked nose, and a gaping mouth.

They went on to the last chamber, a broad space with a low arced ceiling. The water seemed very still, more like a lake than a river.

'This is as far as we can go,' said the guide. 'But divers have discovered many more chambers, including one that's a hundred feet high.'

'Can you swim there?' said Billy.

'You can if you're a very experienced diver.'

Billy stood at the water's edge, gazing into the depths. People had been down there, he thought, explorers. How far could you get? If you went on for long enough surely you would come to the very source of the river. And then beyond that, the centre of the earth. If there was nowhere left to explore above ground, then he could always come to places like this.

He turned around, and saw that he had been left behind. Setting off for the entrance, he cast his gaze back one last time towards the river. And at that moment the lights in the cave went out.

Billy stood immobile, in absolute darkness. He was completely disorientated, and unsure what to do. He took a few halting steps, and then shouted, 'Dad!' His voice echoed around the cave, but there was no answering call. It occurred to him that he should feel afraid, but somehow he didn't. The dark and the silence were magical: he had never experienced such an absence of things. He stretched out his arms and whirled slowly around. What an extraordinary feeling this was, one of complete peace and freedom. He came to a stop, and called his father once again.

He had no idea how long it was before he saw the beam of a torch and heard voices approaching, but he sensed it had been a while.

'I'm here,' he said.

'Where?' said his father's voice.

'Here, somewhere.'

The torch came nearer. 'Bloody electricity cuts,' Billy heard the guide say. 'We just can't have this.'

As they came up to him, he was dazzled by the light.

'What were you thinking of?' said his father. 'Why didn't you keep up?'

'I liked it down here.'

'I don't care how much you liked it. You've given your mother and me the fright of our lives. You have to think of other people. You can't stay in your daydream world all the time.'

Billy stared at his father's face, which was strangely distorted in the torchlight. Who was he to talk about thinking of other people? He felt the grip of Jim's hands on his arms. It was so tight it hurt. And then he noticed that his father's cheeks were wet.

'Did you get dripped on?'

Jim put a hand up to his face. 'Have you never seen a man cry before?' he said.

Billy could only shake his head.

'Well sometimes we do. Just like everyone else.'

★   ★   ★

At school the next morning, Billy found it quite impossible to concentrate. The memory of his adventure in the caves crowded out everything else. Miss Shute gathered together the five children who would be taking the eleven-plus and sat them at the front of the class.

'Today we're going to do equations,' she said. 'Now, does anyone know what an equation is?'

Alan Tyler's hand shot up.

'Yes, Alan?'

'It's a line that goes around the middle of the world, miss.'

'No, that's the *equator*. Anyone else?'

The children's hands stayed down.

'Very well. An equation is something that

equals something else.' She turned to the blackboard and chalked the number four, then a line below it, and below that a two. Then she drew two short parallel lines next to them.

'Four over two equals something, doesn't it, children?' she said. 'What is that?'

They studied the blackboard. It was obvious to Billy that this was as puzzling to everyone else as it was to him.

'Four over two equals two, doesn't it?' said Miss Shute. 'In other words, two *into* four equals two.' She chalked a two on the other side of the parallel lines. 'Now, let's make it a little more difficult, shall we?'

'It's difficult enough already, miss,' said Audrey.

'All will become clear. Now, if I write four over two here, and eight over four there, what does that mean?'

'That four over two equals eight over four,' said Billy.

'Quite right. And why does it?'

Billy looked at the numbers on the board. 'Because four into eight is also two,' he said after a few moments.

'Excellent. So, you see how an equation may balance out numbers that seem much larger and smaller than each other.'

In the playground at morning break Alan

said to the other boys, 'I don't think I get it, this equations thing.'

'But we've only just started,' said Billy. 'We'll get the hang of it.'

'It's all right for you,' said Les. 'You're a swot.'

At this Frank turned on Les. 'No he isn't,' he said. He looked at Billy, and then again at Les, this time with a faintly menacing expression. 'You know what I think?' he said. 'I think Billy Palmer's all right, that's what I do.'

★　★　★

Jim and Liz sat on a bench in the recreation ground, looking across to the bandstand and the deserted croquet lawn. The first shoots of spring were appearing, and the air seemed almost balmy. He had wondered how to do this, whether to take her out one last time, write her a letter, or what. In the end this seemed the best solution. She had a day off from Goody's, and he asked her to meet him here at lunchtime.

'Say it, then,' she said.

'You do understand, don't you?'

'All I understand is that you've had your fun, and now you must run along home to your wife.'

Jim watched the children playing on the swings and slides, wondering how to reply. He heard a little boy say to his mother, 'I want all those other children to get off the roundabout before I get on.'

'I really care for you,' he said finally.

'I hate those words, 'care for',' she said. 'They mean you don't love me.'

'I never said I loved you, Liz. I never used that word, and nor did you.'

She gazed into the distance. 'Do you love your wife?' she said.

'Yes,' said Jim unhesitatingly.

'Then why go looking for someone else? Why chase after me?' She bit her lower lip. 'This was a mistake,' she said.

'I'm sorry. I made it happen.'

She shrugged her shoulders and shifted on the bench.

'Will you say anything to her?'

'No. Why?'

'I don't know. Don't men fall on their knees and confess the error of their ways?'

'Not this one.'

'That sounds cynical.'

'Well it's not meant to be. It's just who I am, that's all. I've never been one for fancy words.'

She stood up, hesitated, and then bent down to give him a kiss on the cheek.

'See you at the first night, then.'

'That's what everyone seems to be saying at the moment.'

She turned and hurried away towards the palace moat. Jim watched her figure recede, and then looked back at the children in the playground. The little boy who wanted the roundabout to himself was sobbing now, his mother trying to calm him. Jim stared beyond them. What has this been about, he wondered, and why is it always this way? Why, when the moment came for parting, did they seem to feel something and he nothing at all? Slowly he raised himself and turned in the opposite direction.

★ ★ ★

'Let's invite Leonora and Hubert to supper,' said Margaret one day as they sat at the kitchen table.

Jim looked at her doubtfully. 'That's the silliest idea I've ever heard,' he said. 'What on earth would they say to each other?'

Margaret shrugged. 'I don't know,' she said. 'But they're both alone, aren't they?'

'They've lived within a stone's throw of each other for ages, and if they had wanted to get acquainted they'd have done so by now.'

'Yes, but it's only a year since Mary Fosse died.'

Jim looked across the yard to the outbuilding where Hubert lived. Perhaps he was being ungenerous.

'Very well,' he said.

She arranged a date for the following week. Billy and Sarah were promised they would be able to stay up at least until their guests arrived, and when the evening came around there was an air of expectancy in the house. Jim set out the bottle of whisky that Leonora had given them at Christmas, which had remained untouched since Hubert's last encounter with it on New Year's Eve.

Hubert wore a clean white shirt that was buttoned up to the neck, and he had shaved for the first time in days; there were nicks and scratches around his chin. As Jim made him a whisky and water, he sat stiffly in the chair staring at his large red hands.

'Have you heard about the new people at Perridge Farm?' said Jim.

'I've heard they plan to bring in Charolais,' said Hubert.

'Charolais?'

'It's a French breed of cattle. Some people seem to have got it into their heads that British breeds won't do.'

'Are French cows better, then?' said Billy.

'They certainly aren't, young man. You can't beat a British cow.'

Leonora had insisted on walking up the hill, and she was wheezing by the time she arrived at the house. Sarah took her coat and scarf, dancing around her in attendance. Since there weren't enough chairs in the parlour, Jim and Hubert came through into the kitchen and everyone sat at the table. Margaret sent Billy and Sarah off to bed, and began to prepare the meal.

'So when did you two last see each other?' said Jim a little too heartily.

'At Mary's funeral,' said Hubert.

'It was a very fine funeral, too,' said Leonora. 'Harry Hardie did her proud.'

'Right he did. He always had a soft spot for her.' Hubert drank his whisky, and Jim took the glass and topped it up.

'How about you, then, Leonora?' said Hubert. 'Life treating you all right?'

'Yes, thank you. My life has improved considerably lately, thanks to my new friends.'

Jim placed a tall white jug in the middle of the table. Hubert grasped it, and then set it down again. Watching him, Margaret recalled that the jug was one of the things that had come with the house.

'Mary used to say it was like a swan,' he said. He took it in his hand again and poured water for the others. 'She loved swans.'

'You used to walk together along the rhynes down at Redlake, didn't you, Hubert?' said Leonora.

'A long time ago, yes. She loved it down there, the marshes and ditches. You'd see bitterns and grebes and mallard ducks, hundreds of them.'

'I expect you still do,' said Jim.

'I haven't been down there for years.'

There was the sound of footsteps on the stairs. Sarah appeared, her nightgown hitched up around her knees, her eyes blinking in the light of the kitchen.

'My leg hurts, Mummy,' she said. 'Can I have some magic cream?'

Margaret went to the cupboard where she kept her hand cream, and sat Sarah on her lap.

'Where does it hurt?'

Sarah thought for a moment, and then pointed at the shin of her left leg. 'There,' she said.

'I get terrible pains in my legs,' said Leonora. 'It's all that dancing I used to do. It's caught up with me.'

Sarah watched her mother rub some cream into her skin. 'How can dancing catch up with you?' she said.

'It's an expression, sweetheart,' said Jim.

'What's an expression?'

'It's a way of saying things,' said Margaret. 'Now, back to bed.'

'But my leg still hurts.'

'Then lie on your other side.'

The evening fell rather flat after Sarah left the kitchen. Hubert cradled his whisky glass, becoming increasingly maudlin. The others tried to find things to talk about, but their consideration for Hubert made them tongue-tied. There was very little to be said that might engage him, and much that might exclude him. In the end Jim took him off to the parlour while Margaret and Leonora remained at the kitchen table.

'He's the loneliest man I've ever known,' said Leonora after they'd gone.

'He's alone.'

She looked at Margaret thoughtfully. 'He's much more than alone,' she said.

★ ★ ★

On the way back to the shop after lunch one day, Jim bought a copy of the *Wells Journal*, and a headline at the bottom of the front page caught his eye. 'Verdicts in Pettigrew Case', it ran. Tony Lewis was lounging outside, and Jim opened up, shut the office door behind him, and sat down to read the story.

'The trial of four men accused of stealing and receiving books owned by Mr Alfred Pettigrew took place this week at Wells Assizes. Mr Justice Bonington handed down sentences on George Crocker, Arthur Trafford and Gordon Towker. Crocker and Trafford were given custodial sentences of twelve months for robbery. Towker was given a three-month suspended sentence for receiving stolen goods. In the case of Bernard Smith, the London bookseller who attempted to sell on the books, the judge stated that there was reasonable doubt as to whether he was aware the books were stolen, but that he should have taken the trouble to inquire as to their provenance. He was let off with a reprimand.

'In the case of Gordon Towker, however, Mr Justice Bonington concluded that he must have known that the books were stolen. Towker will be obliged to report to Wells police station once a month for the next year. In his summing up, Mr Justice Bonington remarked that the fact that none of the men had a previous criminal record had led him to treat them leniently. When contacted by our reporter, Mr Pettigrew pronounced himself satisfied with the outcome, but particularly satisfied that he had recovered all the books in good condition.'

Jim tossed the paper aside, dragged the heavy Olympia typewriter from its shelf, and inserted a piece of Underhill's notepaper into it. Laboriously he began to type. 'To Whom It May Concern,' he wrote. 'Mr Anthony Lewis worked as my assistant in Underhill's Outfitters from January 1958 to March 1959. He was an exemplary employee, hard-working and conscientious, and displayed a keen interest in all aspects of the clothing trade. I would have no hesitation in recommending him to a future employer, and I wish him the best of luck in his future endeavours. James Palmer, Manager.'

He drew the piece of paper out of the typewriter, signed it, and went through into the shop.

'Here,' he said. 'A little billet-doux.'

Lewis took the note from him. 'I didn't think you knew any French,' he said.

'I know a damn sight more than you think.'

Lewis read the reference. 'Very elegant,' he said. 'You should try your hand at writing some time.'

'I'll stay with what I know,' said Jim.

Lewis folded the piece of paper and put it

in the breast pocket of his jacket. It stuck out like a trophy.

'You'll be going now, then,' said Jim.

'Yes, I suppose I will.'

They stared at one another for a few moments. Then just as Jim was about to turn away, Lewis stepped forward and planted a kiss firmly on his lips. Jim reared back, wiping his mouth with the sleeve of his cardigan.

'Bye-bye, Jimmy,' said Lewis. 'Thanks for the memories.'

'Get out,' said Jim, and he strode back into the office.

⋆   ⋆   ⋆

In the weeks since Billy had confronted his father over Liz Burridge he had sensed a distinct change. Jim had not scolded him once, except when he got lost in the caves at Wookey Hole, and even then he'd been crying at the same time. But nor had he really talked to Billy, at least not about anything that mattered very much. His father was distant, bound up in his own thoughts. Was he still seeing that girl, and would his mother find out? He wished there were someone he could confide in.

When Leonora Vale opened the front door of Tanyard Cottage, Billy said, 'I was wondering if you needed any help planting seeds in the garden?'

She looked at him for a few moments. 'Perhaps it's time to take some out of the greenhouse and plant them outside,' she said.

They went through the house to the walled garden at the back. The cats stirred as they passed, and a kitten leaped onto his shorts. Gently unhooking its claws, he set it down on the floor.

The garden was in much the same state as when Billy had last seen it, a sort of garden-in-waiting. Leonora opened the greenhouse door and they stepped inside.

'Now, let me see,' she said. 'I think we'll start with the peonies.'

She handed him a flowerpot and, carrying another herself, led the way to a border of soil that lay beside the wall of the house.

'We'll need a trowel,' she said. 'There's one in the shed.'

He searched among the clutter and found a small spade which he took to be a trowel.

'Now, dig a small hole here, about three inches deep,' said Leonora. She watched as he did so. 'How did you know how much I hate kneeling nowadays?'

Billy took a pot from her and sprinkled some of the seed-laden earth into the hole he had dug. Then he dug more holes and distributed the rest of the seeds among them.

'Pat them down,' said Leonora, 'and spread some of the soil you've dug up over them.'

When the job was done she went into the kitchen to make tea. She gave Billy a glass of milk, and they sat down.

'So,' said Leonora. 'What have you been doing lately?'

'We went to Wookey Hole, to the caves. I got lost in the dark.'

'That sounds very brave.'

'Yes, it was.'

Billy took a gulp of milk and wiped his upper lip. He looked at Leonora hesitantly, and decided that now was the moment to take the plunge.

'You know those seeds we planted,' he said. 'Do they need eggs?'

'Eggs?'

'Yes. I thought seeds went with eggs, that they needed each other to make . . . ' His voice trailed off.

'To reproduce, you mean.'

'Yes, to reproduce.'

Leonora laid down her cup. 'There are different kinds of reproduction, Billy,' she said. 'Plants don't have eggs, only animals.'

'And we're animals, aren't we?'

'We are.'

'So we couldn't do it with just seeds, then,' he said. 'We need seeds *and* eggs.'

She looked at him with a puzzled expression. 'That's right,' she said.

'But wouldn't it be better if we could. I mean, wouldn't it be easier if we didn't need both?'

'That depends,' she said. 'It would certainly be simpler.'

Billy looked at his empty glass. He felt vaguely disappointed by Leonora Vale's response to this problem, and thought it best to leave things there. 'I'd better go home,' he said. 'They'll be expecting me for lunch.'

She saw him to the door.

'Thank you, Billy,' she said. 'You've been a great help.'

'That's all right. It was fun.'

'Perhaps you should be a gardener when you grow up.'

'Oh no, I'm going to be an explorer.'

'Ah. More exciting.'

'Yes, much more.'

★ ★ ★

It was a year since Jim had been declared bankrupt, and he had to report to the County Court in Bath. Margaret went with him, and he was grateful for her company. Except for his passing through on the way to London, he hadn't been back to Bath since they left.

The cavernous room was full of people who were clearly in some sort of trouble, and Jim wished he were not numbered among them. They had to wait a long time, but eventually John Marshall appeared and led them into a small cubicle in which there was just enough space for Jim and Margaret to sit across the desk from him.

Marshall was in his forties. His hair and suit and tie were very black, his shirt and his papery skin very white. He made a show of looking for Jim's file, and opened it carefully. Then he sat back in his chair and smiled at them.

'Thank you for taking the trouble to come,' he said.

Jim remembered him as not a bad sort of bloke. He'd been as accommodating as he could at the time of the proceedings, and had even looked the other way on occasion. His manner was excessively courteous, and it was typical that he should thank Jim for taking the trouble to do something he was legally bound to.

'So how have you been?' said Marshall.

'Fine,' said Jim.

'Now let's see, we last spoke just before you moved to Coombe, and took up the job at Underhill's Outfitters in Wells.'

'In August.'

'And you're still at Underhill's?'

'I'm running the place,' said Jim. 'The proprietor had a stroke towards the end of the year.'

'I'm so sorry. And he's a relative of yours, Mrs Palmer, I believe?'

'He's my uncle,' said Margaret. 'He's been at home for some time now, looked after by his wife.'

Marshall turned to Jim. 'So you have new responsibilities?' he said.

'I do indeed.'

'Good, good,' he said. He looked down at the file again. 'And you're still living at Fosse's Farm?'

'That's right.'

'How are the children taking to the country?'

'Very well,' said Margaret. 'Especially our son.'

'A country childhood is a fine thing,' said Marshall. 'I don't mean . . . well, I don't mean anything really. A country childhood is a fine thing, though.'

'Mr Marshall,' said Jim, leaning forward, 'how long do you think it might be before I can get discharged?'

'Well, as I said at the time, that's

impossible to say. It may be only three or four years, it may be longer.'

'Time off for good behaviour?'

'Something like that. It's a serious thing, bankruptcy. I think you would do well to remember that. It's a breach of trust.'

'I know it's a serious thing,' said Jim, flushing suddenly. 'I knew it at the time, and I know it even better now.'

'I'm sure you do.' He closed the file with an air of finality. 'Until this time next year, then,' he said.

Out in the street, brilliant sunshine lit up the stone of the town.

'Let's go for a walk,' said Margaret.

'I don't know, Maggie. I'm not sure I want to be seen walking around this place.'

She took his hand in hers. 'You've nothing to be ashamed of,' she said. 'Let's go to the river.'

'I know I've nothing to be ashamed of,' said Jim. 'It's other people I'm worried about. 'Breach of trust' indeed. Who does he think he is?'

Margaret squeezed his hand. 'He's just doing his job, that's all.'

'Just doing his job of persecuting people for trying to make the best of themselves.'

They walked towards Pulteney Bridge, and stood looking over the river and the horseshoe of the falls. Margaret turned to face him.

'You still don't really understand, do you?' she said.

'Understand what?'

'Why you failed.'

'I do, Maggie,' he said. 'I understand a lot better than you think.'

'Do you?'

He gazed down into the rushing water below.

'Just because I'm too bloody proud to admit it doesn't mean I don't know I made mistakes. But breach of trust? I won't accept that.'

'Then you must be trustworthy,' said Margaret, a flash of anger lighting up her face.

He looked at her for a few moments, and then twined his arm around her waist. She knows, he thought, of course she does. Knows about Liz, and others before her.

'Yes,' he said softly.

★ ★ ★

Billy had never been to a funeral before, and in the car on the way to London he tried to imagine what it might be like. He conjured up images of long hearses and hundreds of people dressed in black. Not that they themselves were in black, since, as his mother had pointed out, they possessed almost nothing suitable for such an occasion. Billy looked down at the grey flannels his father had given him. They were his first ever pair of long trousers, and they felt very strange: it was almost like being in bed.

'She should count herself lucky we're coming at all,' said Jim.

'Why, Daddy?' asked Sarah.

'Because she wrote me out of her will, that's why.'

'What does that mean?'

'It means she gave all her money to some charity or other.'

Margaret laid a hand on his arm and said, 'Let it be, Jim.'

So that was why his father had been so grumpy these past few days, thought Billy: he must have hoped for some of Aunt Bea's money.

In the chapel in Brompton Cemetery they found themselves among far fewer people than Billy had supposed. He looked around him, and didn't recognize anyone. He knew that Beatrice had never married, and that his father's own parents had died before he was born; but nonetheless it seemed odd that he should know no one here at all.

Above his head a plaque read, 'I am the

resurrection and the life; he who believes in me, though he die, yet shall he live.' The service droned on, and Billy found himself gazing at Beatrice's coffin. Did he believe in heaven, in life after death? He wasn't sure. Jesus had lived on after the crucifixion, but then he was Jesus. Did everyone go to heaven? It would be very full by now if they did. But then most people didn't go to church very often; his own family seemed to go only when they absolutely had to. Could you not go to church and still go to heaven? He decided it would be wise to go at least a few times a year, just in case.

Out in the cemetery fleeting clouds chased the sun, and the wind caught his mother's skirt and lifted it above her knees. They stood over the grave and looked on as the coffin was lowered into the earth. Magpies flitted among the gravestones, playing tag. A stone near Billy bore an inscription that read, 'On earth one gentle soul the less, in heaven one angel more'. That would be how everyone fitted into heaven — they became angels. Frank Willmott had told him there were people who argued over how many angels could dance on the head of a pin. Six, that was what Frank's dad reckoned.

As the gravedigger shovelled soil over the coffin, Billy tried to hold on to his memories of Aunt Bea. The best were the Boat Races and the teas. And then there were the times she came down on the train from London to stay with them, bringing presents whatever the time of year. Since his father had no sisters she was always Aunt Bea, even though she was really a great-aunt. Now there was no one left in his father's family. He looked across at Jim, who stood with his head bowed. Billy could tell he was angry with his aunt; but clearly he was sad too. Anger and sadness seemed to go together so often, he thought.

'Did she leave us anything at all?' he said when they were back in the car.

'Billy, please . . . ' said his mother.

'But I've just remembered: she always said I could have the binoculars.'

'*You'll* be getting a few things, and so will Sarah,' said Jim. 'But not me.'

★   ★   ★

On a blustery morning Jim looked out of the kitchen window and said, 'I feel like going for a walk. Billy, why don't you show me your hiding places?'

Running towards Southey Hill, Billy called to his father to keep up. The rain clouds raced them along Folly Lane and into the wood.

'This is where we play Cowboys and Indians,' he said. 'There's lots of trees to hide behind.'

Even now the wood was dense and green, the ground carpeted with ivy. The deeply rutted track was slippery with mud, and now and again they had to leap over puddles.

'Why do you think this is called Folly Wood?' asked Billy.

'I don't know. Someone must have done something foolish up here.'

'Something foolish?'

'That's what a folly means, a foolish thing. Or it can mean a building that's been made for no reason, like a tower without a castle around it.'

'A foolish tower?'

'But I think it's more likely that someone *did* something foolish here.'

They came out into an open field. Billy looked ahead, and the tor was in sight again. It was always there, Glastonbury Tor: it followed him everywhere he went.

'It's not that far after all, is it?' said his father.

'What?'

'The tor.'

'Not as far as Wookey Hole.'

'How about the weekend after Mum's play, then?'

Billy gazed at it longingly, and then looked up at Jim. That he had so casually suggested this now struck Billy as being just as unfair as his having denied it to him for so long.

'I'm not sure,' he said.

Billy was as astonished by his words as his father clearly was.

'You're not sure? But you've talked of nothing else for ages.'

He stood silent for a few moments, struggling with his strangely conflicting feelings.

'I'll think about it,' he said.

Jim scratched his chin with his fingertips.

'All right, then. You think about it.'

⋆   ⋆   ⋆

'I hate this wig,' said Liz. It was very long and very blonde, and quite altered her looks. 'Do I have to wear it?'

'But that's how Coward saw Sybil,' said Margaret. 'Anyway, you know what they say, gentlemen prefer blondes.'

'If I knew any gentlemen that might be different,' said Liz sourly.

There was less than half an hour to go, and make-up was just about done. Margaret looked in the mirror and told herself for the hundredth time to be steady. This was something they were doing for fun, which would be seen only by their families and friends, but which nonetheless had sorely tested their modest talents. How absurd her daydreams seemed now, her thoughts of a career on the stage, of fame and freedom.

'And as for this ridiculous dress,' said Liz. She stood up and smoothed down the bright red summer outfit she had been given to wear. 'I feel like I'm at Butlins, not in a smart hotel in France.'

'You look fine,' said Margaret. 'Stop fretting.'

'It's all right for you, you're as cool as a cucumber.'

'I'm as wound up as you. I'm just trying to unwind, that's all.'

Liz sat down again and looked unhappily at her reflection in the mirror. 'I'm sorry,' she said. 'I'll shut up.'

'Don't shut up, for goodness' sake,' said Margaret. 'You've got hundreds of lines to speak any minute.'

She touched the black silk of the negligee she would be wearing in the first scene, feeling for the bump that had just recently appeared. Soon, she said to herself. I will tell him soon.

Diana Mogg came into the dressing room and placed her hands on their shoulders.

265

'All set?' she said.

'As set as a jelly,' said Liz.

'Good, good,' said Diana.

Margaret looked up at her. Clearly nothing would be allowed to perturb her invincible calm.

'How are the men?' she said.

'The men are looking very . . . shiny,' said Diana. She smiled at their reflections, and suddenly they were all giggling.

Diana gave them both a peck on the cheek. 'Break a leg,' she said.

★　★　★

There was a buzz of excitement and trepidation in the car.

'How do you feel about Margaret's name being up in lights, Jim?' said Leonora.

'About time too, I say.'

'Will Mummy's name really be in lights?' said Sarah.

'No,' said Jim. 'It's just a way of saying that she'll be on the stage.'

'I've never seen a play.'

'Yes you have. You've seen nativity plays at Christmas.'

'They're not plays,' said Sarah. 'They're just dressing up.'

They dropped Leonora at the theatre and

266

walked to the Underhills' house. Jim pushed the wheelchair on the way back, Reg making odd noises now and then that Winifred interpreted.

'He says this is his first night out in months,' she said.

They waited in the bar, and Jim drank a pint of bitter rather too fast. Billy ran continually to the door of the auditorium to peek at the stage.

'Nothing's happening,' he said.

'I bet a lot's happening behind that curtain,' said Jim.

A bell sounded, and people began to move towards their seats. Billy and Sarah rushed to the front.

'They're numbered,' said Jim. 'We're over here.'

'I won't be able to see,' said Sarah.

'You can sit on my lap, then.'

The lights dimmed and the curtain rose. The set was two balconies side by side, with terrace furniture and bright orange and white awnings. Liz Burridge appeared on one of them, and called back, 'Elli, Elli dear, do come out. It's so lovely.' Jim barely recognized her. Bert Dampler's voice could be heard from offstage saying, 'Just a minute.' After a pause he joined Liz. 'Not so bad,' he said, to which she replied, 'It's heavenly. Look at the lights of that yacht reflected in the water. Oh dear, I'm so happy.'

When Margaret appeared on the other balcony, Sarah whispered, 'That's Mummy.'

'I know it is, sweetheart,' said Jim. 'Now shush.'

It was a strange sensation seeing his wife wearing not very much and being referred to as 'darling' by another man.

'I wish I knew you better,' said Michael Ford.

'It's just as well you don't,' replied Margaret. 'The 'woman' — in italics — should always retain a certain amount of alluring feminine mystery for the 'man' — also in italics.'

'What about the man?' said Michael. 'Isn't he allowed to have any mystery?'

'Absolutely none. Transparent as glass.'

The actors did their best, and there were moments when Jim could imagine that this was something more than a brave and good-natured effort. Margaret held his eye throughout, sometimes for her acting, but mostly because she was his wife. The applause at the end seemed to him to express relief as much as enthusiasm. When Margaret emerged from backstage he gave her a fond embrace.

'You were great,' he said. 'I knew you would be.'

★ ★ ★

Jim needed to do some stocktaking in the shop, and he suggested that Billy come along with him one Saturday morning and spend some time exploring Wells while he worked. It was raining, and a fierce wind was blowing. They passed the Infirmary on the way into town.

'I fancy we'll be spending some time in that place soon,' said Jim.

'Why?'

'I have a feeling your mother has something to tell us. She thinks I haven't guessed, but I have.'

'What?' said Billy, confused now.

'Well, how would you feel about having another brother or sister?'

'Another one? Now?'

'Yes, now.'

Billy gazed out of the window at the windswept streets. This was the last thing he might have expected.

'I'd like a brother,' he said.

'I thought you'd say that.'

'Which would you like?'

Jim sighed. 'Oh, I don't mind,' he said, 'a

boy or a girl. I'll have to make some changes whichever it is.'

'Changes?'

They pulled up outside the shop, and Jim turned towards Billy. 'I'll have to be around a bit more,' he said.

Billy looked back at his father. Why had it taken this news about a new baby for him to say this; why hadn't he said it ages ago?

'That'll be good.'

He spent the morning wandering around the town. With any luck, this would soon be his place too. He stood on the pavement outside the Blue School. It was huge compared to his present school, but still smaller than the Unicorn. He'd get used to it, he was sure.

When his father had finished the stock-taking they had lunch in the Anchor. As they were driving out of the town Jim said, 'We could go now, if you like.'

Billy looked ahead, at the outlines of Glastonbury Tor.

'Yes,' he said. 'Let's go now.'

The hill loomed larger and larger in the windscreen as they approached. It seemed to change shape, too, as though it were a living thing. Eventually it dominated their view, shutting out everything else. Billy craned his neck so as to keep the top of it in sight.

Jim turned into a road that led up the side, and pulled the car over as close to the hedge as possible. Billy raced ahead up the steep slope. As they neared the summit the rain eased, but the cold wind still tore through their coats. Billy ran around the tower, which was all that remained of the church that had once stood there.

'It's freezing up here,' said Jim, wrapping his collar around his chin.

'It's great!' shouted Billy. 'Look, over there is Wells. And that must be where we live, can you see?'

Billy was sure he had never seen anything like it before. This must be the way things looked from an aeroplane. Everything took on a different aspect from up here, everything fitted together in a way that could be understood. To the north lay Wells and the Mendips, with Alfred's Tower beyond, to the west the Bristol Channel, and to the south the flat expanse of the Levels. He tried to point out some of the landmarks, but the wind robbed him of his words.

'Let's go inside,' said Jim. But as they sought shelter, they discovered that the tower acted as a kind of wind tunnel, and they were blown out of the other side. Billy ran around to the entrance again, and this time he careered through, unable to stop himself. Jim tried it too, almost losing his footing as he was swept out of the tower and down the hill. It was exhilarating. They ran through the tower time and again, the wind rushing in their ears, Billy sprawling on the ground and shrieking with laughter.

'Where's the hawthorn bush?' he asked when they were getting their breath back.

'Over there, I think,' said Jim. 'On Wearyall Hill. We'll go there another day, and to the abbey.'

'Oh, I don't care,' said Billy. 'This is the best, the tor.'

They stood for a few moments surveying the landscape, and then Billy broke away to run through the tower once more.